The C
a Brussel:

To Louise & Tommy,

Thanks for bringing us all together again for Christmas.

This wee leabhar comes from Bruxelles with love.

- Paul

Also by the Brussels Writers' Circle:

Circle of Words
Harvard Square Editions, 2016

The Circle
A Brussels Anthology
Edited by Patrick ten Brink
Harvard Square Editions, 2018

The Circle 19:
a Brussels Anthology

Curated by Cynthia C Huijgens

A community literary project of the
Brussels Writers' Circle

Published by Idle Time Press, LLC
USA / EUROPE
2019

Copyright © 2019 Idle Time Press

None of the material contained herein may be reproduced or stored without written permission of the authors under International and Pan-American Copyright Conventions.

Cover Art: Mimi Kunz
Cover Design: Suzana Stankovic

ISBN: 978-1-7329258-0-9

Published by
IDLE TIME PRESS, LLC
www.idletimepress.com

This book is a work of fiction. References to real people, events, establishments, organizations, or places are intended to provide a sense of authenticity and are used fictitiously. All other characters, incidents and dialogue are drawn from authors' imaginations and are not to be construed as real.

INTRODUCTION

Monday to Friday, the city of Brussels is buzzing with politically charged activity, but after hours and at the weekends it's a magical hotbed of diverse, contemporary arts and culture. Hiding in the midst of this creative energy is the Brussels Writers' Circle. The BWC has been meeting weekly above Maison des Crepes, just steps from Brussels' famous Grand Place, for more than a dozen years. The group attracts people of all ages and walks of life, published and emerging writers, poets, screenwriters, playwrights and songwriters.

Writing can be a lonely endeavor, and sometimes a short story or poem can take years to perfect. The BWC is an open platform for any writer, new to Brussels or born and bred, seeking renewal, motivation, inspiration, friendship or reassurance. Writers, sometimes five or six, sometimes twenty, crowd around tables to listen to works-in-progress and share feedback over a pint or two of Belgium's beers. Inevitably, knowledge and insights are exchanged, all in the spirit of helping each other to develop and improve our craft. And then, 'poof', like the best kind of magic from a well-stirred cauldron, published pieces emerge and we celebrate each other's successes.

For many of the eleven poets and fifteen writers showcased in ***The Circle 19: a Brussels Anthology***, English is not their native language. Though their chosen profession may be doctor, engineer, translator, teacher or diplomat, and their genres stretch from science fiction to nonfiction, poetry to children's fairy tales, their contribution hints at the range of talent within BWC and collectively offers a guided tour into the less-travelled, magic-laden parts of Brussels – the parvis after dark, the flat where two lovers quarrel, sun's first cast of silver light, when strangers meet in a crowded cafe.

The Circle 19: a Brussels Anthology is the third publication of literary work by past and current members of the Brussels Writers' Circle. It would not exist without the tenacity and dedication of the Editorial Team. Much gratitude to Patrick ten Brink, Niamh Moroney, Ross Noble, Ocean Smets, Alexandros Yannis, Jay Harold, Antoinette Naomi Reddick, Kevin Dwyer, and Adalbert Jahnz. The team met time and again, sharing drinks and meals while discussing the merits of each submission. Our process went something like: *'read, write, meet, repeat'*, and eleven months later, ***The Circle 19: a Brussels Anthology*** emerged.

A big thank you to BWC member Mimi Kunz for contributing this year's cover art. And thank you to the Brussels-based businesses that support us by selling our books and allowing us to occupy their tables and chairs every Tuesday and Thursday night. Happy Reading!

Cynthia C Huijgens

Creative Director, Idle Time Press

Member, Brussels Writers' Circle, since 2016

CONTENTS

Ann Milton	1	RELEASING A POEM
	2	SILENT STRUGGLE
Martin Jones	4	REMEMBER, REMEMBER
ME Grey	10	FLASHBULB HANDSHAKE
	11	IMPACT PATHWAY METRIC
	12	SCENARIO
Karmen Špiljak	14	THE COLLECTORS
Paula Dumont	28	BLAZER MAN
Niamh Moroney	36	AH YEAH!
	39	SOAK, A POEM FOR CONOR
	41	TAT
Roumiana Karapetrova	45	BREATH
	46	BEGGAR
	47	CHOICES
Andrea Rees	48	THE COMMUTE
	53	TRUE LOVE
Zoheb Mashiur	54	BRAND NEW ME
Jay Harold	69	ROSABELLE AVENUE
	70	WIVENHOE DREAMING
Irina Papancheva	72	SAUDADE
TD Arkenberg	83	PARVIS DE SAINT-GILLES
Dimitris Politis	100	ALL THE MOTHERS OF THE WORLD
Teodora Lalova	106	ONE SPRING
Larisa Doctorow	108	THE IMMORTAL REGIMENT
Sean Gibson	115	HOW LONG IS LONG ENOUGH
	116	SHE TOLD ME SO
	117	CHILDREN

Manuel Delgado	118	BIRTHDAY IN HER EYES
	119	WAR AT SWEET NIGHTFALL
Alexandros Yannis	120	THE WAR AND THE WALL
Xavier Queipo	129	KOTARO
	131	ME NOT DARING TO TALK TO YOU
Katja Knežević	133	THE DINNER
Anastasia Cojocaru	148	TEDDIES
Sheila Kinsella	150	IN MARY SCHOLES' HOUSE
Klavs Skovsholm	158	A PIRATE PARROT CHRISTMAS
Patrick ten Brink	168	THE CARP AND THE MAGPIE
Jeannette Cook	182	DEER OF EUROPE
	183	MAELBEEK STATION, SHORTLY AFTERWARD
	184	STILL HERE

Ann Milton
RELEASING A POEM

Words struggle out

twisting

pulsing onto the vacant

white page

where space embraces the

black marks

blending them into a mosaic

of truths

that escape all my best designs.

Phrases evolve as

my off-spring develop

linking

those once unrelated words

which

I guide but cannot control.

Dreams

that were once my children

now

have a life of their own.

SILENT STRUGGLE

Serene grey moon
governs the night,
resisting dawn as it
threads over roofs,
weaving light through trees.

Slowly the dull clouds
that defined the night
bleach to cream as they
draw close to Earth
shrouding the land with their mist.

Moon loses its dominance but
Sun has not claimed her place;
through pale silhouetted trees
Dawn struggles until
monochrome night
retreats.

Slowly, irreversibly,
whilst the sun remains in wait,
Dawn wins through the mist.
Night's silver is forfeit as
sunlight floods the day.

Ann Milton was born in England and raised and educated in London and Belgium. She has lived in Brussels for 25 years, working as a wife and mother, and in various voluntary roles including spiritual direction and conversation with the blind. She also enjoys singing, walking and visiting London. Her time abroad has developed her passion for the English language.

Martin Jones
REMEMBER, REMEMBER

My doctor told me to write stuff down, said it would help me. Something about 'gaining a locus of control over unresolved past experiences related to infantile psychosexual impulses and behaviours'. She said I should find a spot where I feel comfortable and can 'maintain a positive reinforcement of my legitimate needs'. Whatever that means. I suppose she meant somewhere quiet. So, no quieter place than the library. No one ever goes in there.

Looking out the window, the grounds were wreathed in mist. Pine trees obscured the wall as dark, jagged shapes. Funny how things change. When I was growing up, spring was my favourite season. As a young man, that changed to summer. Now it's autumn. I suppose when I start looking forward to winter, that'll be it.

I jerked the window open, just to savour those wonderful tangy, musty smells of autumn. That's when I smelt the bonfire. Images of my childhood rushed back. You never smell bonfires in autumn any more. They've probably been made illegal by some locust-eyed sanctimonious zealot in the name of public safety. Good word, zealot. Mind you, I've always been good with words.

Craning out of the window I could see the gardener. He was raking the leaves into a pile and putting them in a wheelbarrow. He wheeled them over to the bonfire and forked them on. The wet leaves seemed to dampen it down for a bit, then caught in gouts of smoke. I leant out to get a closer look. The gardener put his hand on his back and straightened up. I could almost hear his bones creak. He was getting on. Sixty, at least. Glancing up, he saw me. He didn't say anything, but looked at me suspiciously. Can't say I altogether blame him given the circumstances. Anyway, I'm getting off track. Like I said, the doctor asked me to write about it. To be honest, I struggle to remember some of the details. Not all of them, of course. But it seems like such a long time ago now.

It all started when that little runt began working at the council offices. My wife worked there too. When she came in that night bubbling with excitement, her eyes all shiny, I knew something was amiss.

"What do you think," she said. "Peter has come to work at my office."

"Who's Peter?" I said, appearing more interested in the telly. Funny how I remember that.

"You remember. I told you about him. We were at school together. We used to go out," she said, going pink.

"Really?" I said. I didn't take much notice to be honest. She'd always been a bit of a flirt at parties when she spoke to a man, she was all wide-eyed and, well, you know how women get, like he's the only person in the room. I had hated it at first, like she was doing it to taunt me about my problem, but you get used to stuff, don't you?

She went on, 'Peter said this, Peter did that, oh, he's so funny'.

Now I was beginning to pay attention. "Is he?" I said, all cold. Anyway, it shut her up and she went off to do the washing-up, crashing around like she was angry.

The next day she didn't mention Peter, nor the day after. Anyway, I was busy at work. We had had problems with a missing order and they blamed me for it. I hate that. Well, I forgot all about him. Almost.

Where she works at the Council, they had a summer picnic every year. They were Lib-Dem then. All touchy-feely. Supposed to promote team bonding or some such rubbish. They kept on about it being a tradition. Right. Trooping the colour, that's tradition, not some stupid picnic. As usual, she dragged me along, and as usual, halfway through, it pissed down with rain. But I noticed him, the little squirt. He was totally nondescript, thinning hair and steel rimmed glasses. My wife hardly spoke to him. That was when I started to worry.

She was dead quiet all the way home. When she was putting our tea in the microwave, I confronted her, "Don't be silly," she said. She would say that, wouldn't she? I decided best to keep an eye on her.

She didn't mention him again for a couple of months, then we were watching a film on the telly, can't remember the name, it had that actor in it, Jude Law.

"Don't you think Peter looks like that actor?" she said.

I looked at her incredulously.

"No. Jude's twenty years younger and good-looking."

"Oh," she said, quietly.

But that was when I knew.

A week or so later I came home early one night and there was a strange car parked in the driveway. I pulled over on the other side of the street and waited. Not for long. The door swung open and there he was. I watched my wife kiss him. It was only a peck on the cheek but it didn't fool me. He got into his car and drove off as she stood on the doorstep, waving. I waited for a few minutes and then came in.

"Had a good day?" I said, all non-committal.

"Yes. Peter gave me a lift home. He came in for a cup of tea. You don't mind, do you?"

"Not at all," I said, "Why would I?" I kissed her on the top of her head.

This was in the beginning of November. In the village where we live, they have a bonfire every Guy Fawkes Night. It's a big do. Sausage rolls, tomato soup, I expect you know the sort of thing. The local Round Table spends weeks getting it ready. They stack a pile of wooden pallets two or three stories high, smack in the middle of the village green, and then stick a life-size Guy on top. Like I say, it's a big do around here.

Anyway, we spent the evening watching telly. I kept an eye on her, but she never let on. Women are clever like that. We drank our tea and watched the news. Then she said she was going-up and was I coming?

"No," I said, "I've got a bit of a headache. Perhaps I'll go out for a drive. Clear my head." She looked at me funny and then shrugged. "Alright then," she said.

I got into the car and drove to Peter's house. I waited outside. The house was dark. I knew he lived alone. Julie, that's the wife, told me as much. It was cold in my car. I did think about going home, and then I thought, why not? I walked up to the door, rang the bell, and waited. After a while a light switched on. Soon after, the door opened. There was Peter standing in a shabby old dressing gown, blinking at me through those stupid glasses. "Can I come in?" I asked, and pushed past him before he could answer. He didn't protest, just looked at me. He seemed so passive, which is probably what set me off. What happened next is a blur. He must have hit his head on the radiator because he was lying on the floor with a stupid expression on his face and a dent in his forehead the size of a biscuit. And he wasn't breathing.

I was just going to leave him there, but then I had a brilliant idea. I've always been known for my sense of humour.

He was heavier than he looked, but I got him into the back of my car. I drove straight to the village green. It was pretty late now, about half past two. All the houses around the green were in total darkness. I clambered to the top of the bonfire and pulled Guy down. He didn't weight much, made of straw. I took off the mackintosh, wellingtons, and wide brimmed hat, and strewed the straw over the palettes. I managed to get the clothes onto Peter. That was the easy part. Getting him to the top of the pile was a real struggle.

Halfway I nearly gave up, but I knew if I'd quit I'd come over as a right twat, so I struggled on. When we reached the top, he looked pretty good, just like the real Guy, maybe even better.

The next day was bonfire night. I wondered if my wife would mention that Peter wasn't at work but she didn't say anything. Didn't want to give herself away, I suppose.

The day was filled with the usual. Lots of excited kids running around, a beer tent, hamburgers with soggy onions. I drank down a couple of pints, couldn't help looking around, to see if anyone noticed anything. When it was good and dark, someone lit the fire. It was slow going until someone threw petrol over it. The pallets went up with a whoosh. That was when the whole thing really kicked off. No one would know that Peter was dead. But turns out he wasn't. After a slow crackling minute, he began to scream. Freaked out the entire village, I can tell you. Me included. They still talk about it, even after all this time, apparently.

Outside, the gardener had disappeared. Gone to get his dinner, I suppose. It's shepherd's pie today, my favourite. I stuffed my notebook into my pocket. I think the doctor is right. Writing does help. I feel a lot better now.

Martin R. Jones lives in Brussels with his wife and children. He is the author of award-winning short stories and flash fiction. He has written two novellas, a feature-length screenplay and is currently revising his second novel; a thriller set in Malta in the 1930s. A detective novel is in the works.

ME Grey
FLASHBULB
HANDSHAKE

Someone who someone you know knows
meets someone you have not met but who
you have got to know a little bit about
without ever actually enquiring.
They have a photo taken together, to publicly mark
the occasion of their private meeting
on a subject that you know quite a bit about.

Those other things you passively know
– a little workplace leching, a couple
of affairs, certain property holdings;
certain acts of principle which have pissed off
other people with other principles;
certain compromises of which you do not approve
but the only thing worse than compromise is impasse –

have nothing to do with the matter
which they are meeting to discuss

IMPACT PATHWAY METRIC

> (A neighbour at the business network dinner)

What comes after 5G? Someone
at Huawei is leading a team
addressing this question. He is
talking to Philips, to regulators, to many
different people. He is
a smoker, not very mobile.
He will contribute to a step
in a process that will define
interoperability
that will be used around the world and be
the basis for further steps. He is
unlikely to walk them himself.

SCENARIO

          knowing
that medicinal products are
active substances, should be
disposed of correctly, returned
to a pharmacy, not released
into our surroundings

          being
a hoarder, prevaricator,
simply busy

          running
into things – literally; Hirudoid
for the bruising, Tramadol
for the pain; all the relics
of your minor ailments:
expired, or for circumstances
no longer applicable

          moving
apartment again, leaving packing
too late;

              needing

to be more ruthless

with objects;

              throwing

unused medicines in the fifth black bin bag

              knowing

yourself

to be riding the now

and failing the future

M. E. Grey is a British-origin poet based in Brussels. *Pages of an Autumn Journal,* a sequence of poems engaging with public and private events during the turbulent months of late 2016, can be read at www.autumnjournal.eu. More information can be found at www.megrey.eu.

Karmen Špiljak
THE COLLECTORS

From: Theodor.windman@vub.ac.be

To: Gregory.Mason@vub.ac.be

Date: 20 May 2018, 14:10

Gregster!

I made it to Austria. Loved the schnitzel btw! Thanks for the tip. I would have fallen straight into a food coma if it weren't for the schnapps.

The locals are friendly, but not very helpful. No one seemed to understand what I was saying. Some grandma was even shaking her head. She probably thought I was gonna climb the mountains in flip-flops or something.

Bad news about the second half of that Alex Schmidt article: I Googled like crazy, but didn't find it. Nor Alex Schmidt, for that matter. Let's hope he didn't have the same idea as us, so we can claim all the fame & glory.

How's your leg btw, I still can't believe you're missing this (schnitzel, man!). No more vodka Jello shots for you. Maybe you're just getting old ;)

Not sure how much signal there will be up there, but I'll drop you a line when I'm back in town. Shouldn't take more than a few days. Fingers crossed!

Cheers,

Theo

From: Gregory.Mason@vub.ac.be
To: Theodor.windman@vub.ac.be
Date: 20 May 2018, 18:23

Nerdo!

Me and my leg are fine. The cast is actually quite handy when you need somewhere to rest an ashtray or hang a coat or you're looking for an excuse to get out of washing dishes.

Can't believe a schnitzel knocked you down! You'd starve in the wild, LOL. Don't even try something more hard core like a knödel. It's a bread dumpling that might kill you.

Fuck Alex Schmidt! I was really hoping you'd get further with that article than me (seriously – only a paper version in this day & age?) You wouldn't believe the shit our librarian gave me for not reporting 'vandalism', as she called it. As if I was the one who'd torn half of it out and then sent a virus to their archive.

Why would they order only one copy, anyway? I hope whoever took it isn't doing research about Neolithic mass graves or skeletons without broken shinbones.

Take it easy on that schnapps, Nerdo. You know you can't handle liquor and I don't want to fundraise to get your skinny ass back home. We'll have a proper pub-crawl when you're back.

I know you'll be off the grid, but I'll be sending some useful stuff I found today. For starters, I've added a few sentences to our research proposal – see what you think:

All the evidence found in Neolithic mass graves demonstrates ancient beliefs in life beyond death. In killings to acquire territory, the soldiers would break the shins of their victims, in order to prevent them from returning as ghosts. However, recent excavations in Germany and Austria prove not all dead bodies had broken shins. We can therefore assume this belief was not widely shared.

Break a leg ;)

Greg

P.S. Your mum called again. Maybe let her know you're alive? While you're at it, try to get her to send more of that salami. Think of your poor flatmate with the broken leg.

<attachment: Anthropology of death, research methodology.pdf>

From: Theodor.windman@vub.ac.be
To: Gregory.Mason@vub.ac.be
Date: 21 May 2018, 07:04

Finally, I got some signal. Only took me half an hour of walking around in the middle of nowhere. Rock and grass and grass and rock. Feels almost as if I'm on another planet.

Speaking of which, you should have seen the locals I'm crashing with. Chris and Sandra would look great on the cover of Stephen King's Misery. She has that bewildered Kathy Bates look and cuts her own hair, and he's always scribbling something. She's also obsessed with cooking. Not sure how much more I can eat, but I guess I'll find out.

Chris knows some guy who dug out bones a while ago (not as a hobby, I hope). I'll stick around to see if he knows anything. I've tried to bring up the ghost village story but all Chris and Sandra want to talk about is food. Maybe I have to get them drunk (we did say we wanted fresh and creative methodology, right?)

If I don't get anywhere in the next two days, I'll go back. Tomorrow, Sandra is making her famous soup. She goes on and on about it, some kind of national dish or something. No knödel in it, I checked. Thanks for the stuff you sent. I'll take a closer look when I get back to civilisation.

Cheers,

Theo

<attachment: location Theo Windman.jpg>

From: Gregory.Mason@vub.ac.be
To: Theodor.windman@vub.ac.be

Date: 22 May 2018, 14:08

Smells like a Fulbright scholarship (unless that Sandra woman plans to keep you and feed you till you become a sumo fighter)!

If you do find that bone guy, go by the book and leave the digging to the pros. You wouldn't want to mess up the material by accident.

The map you sent makes no sense. There's nothing there: the closest village is like an hour's hike away. Sure your GPS wasn't off?

BTW, I finally got news about Alex Schmidt (and I now get why we couldn't find him). It's not a *him*, it's a *her*. Can you believe it? Alex is short for Alexandra. No one knows where she went after her Erasmus.

Keep me posted,

Greg

From: Gregory.Mason@vub.ac.be
To: Theodor.windman@vub.ac.be
Date: 24 May 2018, 01:12

Theo,

Everything OK up there? Tried to call you but it says your number can't be reached. Did you forget to pay the bill again?

Lucky you! I'd love to have someone to cook for me, too. I guess you've headed back already. Have fun with your locals, and let me know when you're at the airport (and call your mum – she called three times today!)

See you in four days. Don't miss your flight!

Greg

From: Fiona.Windman@gmail.com
To: Gregory.Mason@vub.ac.be
Date: 27 May 2018, 14:05

Dear Gregory,

I tried calling you today, but you were busy. Any news from our Theodor? He was supposed to come home, but we haven't heard anything from him. Did he mention visiting any friends? I can't get him on the phone. I am, quite frankly, beside myself. He's never disappeared like this before.

His bill has been paid now (thanks for the scan). I've called the police. If you hear from him, please call me immediately on +44 797 130019.

Regards,

Fiona

From: Gregory.Mason@vub.ac.be
To: Fiona.Windman@gmail.com
Date: 27 May 2018, 21:45

Dear Mrs Windman,

I'm sorry I've missed your calls –I forgot my phone in the office. As said, I haven't heard from Theo since 21 May: he was still in the Austrian mountains and was doing well. I attach the map he sent.

He didn't mention seeing friends. It could be that he found something useful for our research and decided to stay longer? The signal in the mountains is usually quite bad.

He'd been staying with two people called Sandra and Chris (in case it helps).

Tomorrow we have a meeting with our mentor, so I hope to see him there. There's a chance he'll fly in and come directly there. I'll call you the minute I know more. I'll talk to the police today.

Best regards,

Greg

<attachment: location Theo Windman.jpg>

From: Gregory.Mason@vub.ac.be
To: SOS_rescue@bergen.at
Cc: Fiona.Windman@gmail.com, Theodor.windman@vub.ac.be
Date: 28 May 2018, 13:02

Dear Sir/Madam,

My friend, Theodor Windman, went missing in the Austrian mountains on 21 May 2018.

He's 27, about 180 cm tall, skinny and has short brown hair and green eyes (recent photo attached). He was most likely wearing mountain shoes, a dark blue winter jacket and a grey hat. He's a British citizen, studying in Brussels.

His trip was part of our academic research on Neolithic mass graves. His plan was to visit several places to collect the data.

The last time I heard from him, he was staying with two locals (Sandra & Chris - see attached his last location).

His return ticket was never used and neither I, nor his mother (in cc), were able to reach him. The police have been informed and are in touch with Austrian authorities.

Thank you for any information you have.

Best regards,

Gregory Mason

<attachment: location Theo Windman.jpg>

<attachment: Theo Windman photo.jpg>

From: SOS_rescue@bergen.at
To: Gregory.Mason@vub.ac.be
Cc: Fiona.Windman@gmail.com,
Theodor.windman@vub.ac.be
Date: 29 May 2018, 10:41

Herr Mason,

Thank you for your email. Unfortunately, we haven't been able to locate Theodor Windman or get any information on his whereabouts.

The location you sent us hasn't been inhabited for the past 50 years. Even though three old cottages still exist in the area, no one lives there. However, there is a similar case in our database dating back 7 years: a journalist went missing at more or less exactly the same location. His name is Christopher Stieglitz.

His wife requested to be informed in case of similar events, as she might be able to help. With her consent, I enclose her contact details (MariaStieglitz@reflext.at), should you want to get in touch for more information.

We will inform you of any developments.

Mit freundlichen Grüßen,

Heinrich Puller

SOS rescue Austria

From: Gregory.Mason@vub.ac.be
To: Fiona.Windman@gmail.com
Date: 31 May 2018, 21:45

Dear Mrs Windman,

I'm sorry for not answering your calls. I need to see what I can find out about Theo, so this morning I flew to Vienna.

Please don't worry about me. My leg is much better and I've been to Austria before. Tomorrow morning I'll head into the mountains. There is a cable car that can get me to the mountain from the village where Theo was last seen.

I also wrote to a woman named Maria Stieglitz and sent her all the information we have. I hope she can help us find Theo.

I hope to return with good news.

Best regards,

Greg

From: MariaStieglitz@reflext.at
To: Gregory.Mason@vub.ac.be
Cc: Fiona.Windman@gmail.com
Date: 2 June 2018, 15:06

Dear Gregory,

Thank you for your kind email.

As you know, my husband, Chris, disappeared in the mountains while doing research for his book about local folklore. He was especially interested in folk tales about a ghost village. He never finished it.

Chris was in contact with the archaeological institute about evidence on bodies without broken shins. I used to think that his theory about murdered villagers' ghosts seeking revenge was just a tale. I do not think that anymore.

About five years ago, another student got in touch with me, also from Brussels. She was very keen to get there first and wouldn't wait a few days for a local mountaineer. She lost her phone at exactly the same location where my Chris and your friend were last seen. Her name was Alexandra (Sandra) Schmidt. It might be worth getting in touch with her.

I understand you're concerned about your friend's disappearance. However tempted you are to go and search for him, please do not go on your own! In the past fifty years around a dozen people have gone missing there. According to folklore, the ghosts of murdered villagers can only avenge their deaths by collecting souls and increasing the number of ghosts.

If you decide to go against my advice, please do not eat anything once you're up in the mountains. After going through my husband's findings, I have reason to suspect that those who disappeared were poisoned.

I wish you all the best,

Maria

Karmen Špiljak is a Slovenian-Belgian writer and the author of *A Perfect Flaw*. Her short stories have been long-listed in various contests. She lives in São Paulo, where she's working on a novel and a collection of crime stories. When not writing, she runs an offshoot of Brussels Writers' Circle. Find out more on www.karmens.net.

Paula Dumont
BLAZER MAN

It was in that American bar, the Bedford, where I saw him. It must have been only hours before, I even witnessed part of it. Of course, at the time I had no idea. In fact I still don't, not really.

As it had been snowing heavily since early morning, I closed up early. Nobody's going to buy art when they have to concentrate on staying on their feet, are they? On my way home I decided to stop at the Bedford to warm up by the fire with a glass of their excellent single malt.

The weird thing is that I've always said this bar looks like the set of a 1950s spy movie: dark low ceilinged rooms with comfortable armchairs and side tables with the cozy reading lamps. The old black and white photographs of men in aviator uniforms on the walls, that fabulous S-curved counter with a smoky glass mirror behind it and the barman in his dinner jacket and white gloves. The place is like a time warp. Plus the fact that you have to know where to find it. Taking that narrow passageway which leads you off the street onto the courtyard where it's tucked away in the left hand corner. It always gives me a thrill. It's also why I started playing that silly spying game. I choose a spot where I can watch the other guests without being in full view myself, and then I try to guess who they are and why they are there and sometimes I even listen in. I know it sounds creepy, but it was just a bit of innocent fun, until that day.

I arrived well before the after-work crowd would be flooding in and found it almost empty. Having ample choice of seating I went for a chair near the hearth where a fire was crackling away and from where I also had a good view of the counter, on the corner of which a man in a dark blue pinstripe suit was sitting, staring morosely into his drink like some disillusioned hero from a film noir. Two stools down, a couple was facing each other rather closely. Ordering at the counter I'd been able to study them from up close.

Pinstripe Suit, I guessed was in his late thirties or early forties. He had a clear-cut profile with a prominent nose; clean-shaven with thick dark wavy hair, which gave him that old fashioned look that I needed him to have. He wore his bespoke suit with the right kind of shoes, black, shiny brogues and not those paleish brown ones that are currently in fashion. I took him for a banker but he could certainly have played the part of a spook from the cold war era. Plus you could say that in some way bankers have a licence to kill.

The man of the couple was well into middle age if not past, stout with a fleshy face and hair that was thinning out. He wore a blazer, grey flannel trousers and a garishly striped shirt with a silk scarf. Former captain of industry seemed to be tattooed on his forehead. The woman was a curvy blonde, half his age, as if she could have been anything else, her black dress was giving the man full view of her impressive cleavage and from where I was sitting, it seemed he was preparing to plunge into it head first. They were drinking the same ridiculously coloured cocktails, which apparently were a great source of amusement for them. Giggling and cooing, they were disturbing some of the other customers. At that time of day, the bar is more a place for hushed conversation. Two women sitting on the other side of the fireplace, who were having what looked like a business meeting, sighed with irritation.

I gave them a glance of commiseration because I felt it was expected of me, but then my attention went back to Pinstripe suit. There was something odd about him and it took me a while to realise what it was. He just sat there on his own, doing nothing. Nobody does that anymore. Whenever people arrive somewhere on their own, they immediately get out their phone. Those who, like me, prefer reading a newspaper or a book are becoming rarer by the day. And he was not doing that either, nor did he have a chat with the barman, which is another thing people sitting on their own at a bar do.

I wondered, was this man depressed? Had he been let go? Perhaps that was why he had no phone. He had to hand it in together with the keys of the company car. He hadn't touched his drink since I arrived so he was not on a drinking spree. I was starting to enjoy myself but it was not until I noticed that every now and then he looked up into the mirror to glance furtively at the couple next to him, that I became really intrigued.

He was observing them, like I him but unlike me, he was not doing it for fun. My first thought was, is he their bodyguard? But he looked far too posh for that. Was he perhaps listening in? But then what could possibly be of any interest to anyone there, unless he was a private detective working for a jealous spouse. Blazer Man's wife? At their age, after years of marriage wouldn't the wife be used to it and even happy not to have to oblige anymore? It was much more likely to be Blondie's husband. Assuming there was one of course.

But again he seemed far too smartly dressed for a P I. Not that I've ever met one but, you know, in films and books. Anyway, I was just abandoning that theory as well when I thought I saw a glance being exchanged between Pinstripe Suit and Blondie. So, I kept my eyes on her for a while and sure enough there it was again. So now I was no longer entertaining myself with scripts for B-movies. There was really something going on there.

I became aware of an interesting shift in my perception of things. Where before I had supposed I was watching a couple flirting, now it looked like some kind of trap was set up for Blazer man, until then it had seemed to be a classic case of power eroticizes. Everything about him seemed to shout, "Look how important I am." And I had assumed that Blondie, who had looked so obviously up for it, was duly impressed. I'd already catalogued them as rather pathetic. So I clearly had to think again where she was concerned.

Blondie and Pinstripe Suit, could they actually be spooks? Well, it was not that long ago that some Russian was poisoned in a hotel not far from here. Of course they could also be hustlers, trying to get their hands on the man's money. Whatever it was, Blazer Man was definitely of some importance to them. Men like him do tend to sit on half a dozen boards. He might be able to influence some decision or other. Or he could be a politician with something to hide, or perhaps he was a member of some secret society like the freemasons, but more dangerous. The possibilities were endless and I was now totally set on finding out more. However, simply observing them from where I was sitting was not going to get me much further. I decided to go and sit at the counter and have another drink.

Just as I picked up my things and was ready to move, a large group entered the bar and settled themselves at the counter, not only colonising all the available stools but also obscuring my view. I fell back into my seat and for a minute I did not know what to do. I remember thinking 'game over', when I saw Blondie going in the direction of the Restroom, as they call it, followed by Pinstripe Suit. This was my cue.

I pushed the leather-clad door open and entered the antechamber, all marble and mirrors. I did not even have to look around to find them, standing in a corner. They stopped talking the second I came through the door, but their body language echoed the tension of the conversation I had interrupted. I kept my eye on them while I pretended to be choosing something from the bowl of sweets on the table between the doors leading to the Ladies and Gents. He had her literally cornered; only she was slightly taller than him and was looking over his shoulder, straight at me. For a moment I froze, unable to free myself from her gaze. Then nervously, I grabbed a packet of mints and went through to the Ladies where I locked myself in.

I registered the drumming of my heart with a weird sense of detachment, wondering what it was I was afraid of. Surely I did not expect Blondie or Pinstripe Suit to come looking for me. But I did. I was listening for the swinging sound of the door and for the cubicle doors being pushed open one by one. At that point somebody did come in. Heels clicking on the tiled floor, stopping somewhere in the middle of the room. Then nothing. I imagined Blondie looking at the closed door behind which I was hiding and I cursed myself. Why had I not just turned on my heel? I could have been outside, crossing the courtyard, the main street in sight. But then I pictured them coming after me. I could see myself lying face down in the snow, blood slowly spreading around my body.

"Oh stop, stop it." I must have said that out loud because the person on the other side giggled in response. Then I heard water running, the heels again and the swing of the door. Feeling rather stupid now, I turned the lock and stepped into the room. The mirror reflected me looking slightly disheveled, clutching my coat, hat and scarf as if they would shield me. "From what?" I asked my mirror image. *Too much imagination, is not good for you*, my father used to say, and for once I had to agree with him.

But then two days later it was all over the news. How a Belgian Royal had been found on a bench in St James' park, frozen to death, like a homeless person. Seeing his picture on the front page there was no mistaking him, this was Blazer Man. So, no captain of industry former or otherwise. Still, I wasn't far off the mark. Apparently he was a bit of an embarrassment to his family and his country. Always setting-up fraudulent business deals.

As the postmortem was inconclusive there was a lot of speculation about how he ended up dead, and of course, who was responsible. It turned out he had given the Belgian security people the slip and had been missing for 48 hours before he was found. Tabloids had a field day with that. Lots of political finger pointing went on, the Foreign Secretary calling it a major diplomatic incident. And of course people were asked to come forward. They particularly wanted to talk to a blonde woman he'd been seen with. No mention of Pinstripe Suit, however.

For several days I'd been pondering whether I should make that call and if so, what I would say, when they both walked into my gallery. It was late, just before closing time, and of course there was nobody else around. They pretended to be interested in an artist who was not on show, but whose work I've sold in the past. They were being perfectly charming and they were very well informed, very well informed indeed. Needless to say, I never made that call.

Paula Dumont was born in Antwerp and lives with her husband and cat in Schaerbeek. She's an art historian currently working with the Brussels Heritage Department. Paula is a writer and editor of non-fiction and writes short stories in English and Flemish.

Niamh Moroney
AH YEAH!

And poor aul George is dead.
Mmm.
Remember him?
Yeah.
Good aul craic.
Now and then.
A bit weird though.
Ah yeah.
Odd, he was.
The poor aul sod.
I rarely saw him.
It's like he's not gone.
But he is.
Oh he is.

You know I met him on the bus once.
Yeah?
Yeah.
From Cork to Dublin.
Long aul journey.
We sat together,

chatted for hours.

I even took his number.

Oh?

Yeah.

We met up a couple of times.

Right.

The chats got too intense though.

He'd obviously been through quite a lot.

God…

Yeah.

And then he just avoided me…

Why?

Don't know.

Ah, I suppose we'd still say hi,

but no more tight squeeze hugs or

"how are ya love, ya goin for a pint?"

Then I just seen the black ribbon on his front door.

Don't know who his family are,

and I heard nothin' more.

Right.

Yeah.

Do ya think…?

What?

Huh?

Ah nothin'

Hmm...

Hmmm.

SOAK *a poem for Conor*

We took a vow of silence
as we walked to the forest.
Following a trail in one big loop.
Around the Earth in the small wood.

We dined on birdsong.
Danced a carpet of abundant berries.
Flowed with the river.
Clambered up the welcoming trees,
like beasts.

No one else,
just you and me.

Painted in the woodland colours,
our bodies sat at nightfall.
We pushed timber against timber to make heat,
recalled the crackling of spinning records
imitated by our fire.
Turning in to ourselves
we meditated.
I dipped deep into the transcendental pool
visualising golden spirals.

My gut glowed.

Then, my eyes opened against the dark.
And I cried for your brother, my brother,
the leaves on the oak tree.
I couldn't stop!
And hard as I tried,
I couldn't reach out to touch you and say:
Thank goodness!
If only you knew! you would be crying too.

Dawn breaks.
Shoulders tickled by dew.
Giggles bubble up.
Semitones of happiness.
You had come to say goodbye.
The acorns become you.

TAT

Click clack-
She wiggles along.
Tick tack-
her nails tap each other every single time
she inhales her cigarette.
Smick smack-
her lips clap
as she leans in...
"Ah jaysus love yer car's been clamped!"
I shrug, so bloody hungover I'm holding in my sobs.
"Ya know that's a fine of 100 quid?"
I nod.
She stands at the passenger window,
Glancing to the side
I can only see her torso.
She's shiteing on about this that-
the crooked truth.
Spinning me yarns, that don't charm.
Taking long, deep drags on her fag.
My teeth grind,
her nylon coat scrapes against her pleather handbag
shrieking out their plastic sounds.

This honest woman.

Click clack tick tack smick smack
Draaaaaaaag

Made out of tat
Fake lashes, nails, hair extensions.
Dressed from heel to head in knock-off Yves Saint Laurent.
Nothin' real-
only herself,
buried in crusts of fake tan.

Drrrrrrraaaaaaagg
She points.
"D'ya see yer man? D'ya see him?"
"No", I says.
Not even bothering to look.
"Good", she says, "yer not supposed ta!".
"He's got a fine big jackhammer love",
"Wha?"
"He'll drill that stupid clamp clean off"
"Oh!"
The pleather scraping plastic makes me squirm-
I squint
"Can I've a fag?" I ask,
gripping the steering wheel of my static motor,

knuckles white,
pocket full of cash,
...but
A hundred now owed to the council of Dublin.
"Jaysus yeah, here" she says,
handing me an already lit *Carrolls*
A kiss of her pink lippy to greet me.

Click clack tick tack smick smack
Drraaaaaag

Then in a gentle hushed tone:
"C'mere, d'ya want two hundred fags for forty quid?"
"Do I what!?" I beam!
And for a second I dream of smoking each and every single one.
We toke in unison.
Drraaaaaag
I hand her the 40,
with my hand on the 200.
Our eyes glare,
a short distance intensive stare.
"Alright hun?" we simultaneously let go.
Drraaaaagg
"Alright love thanks"
"Okay see ya now".

She wiggles along,
Tick tack her nails
inhaling her cigarette
This honest woman
Gripping the wheel of a static motor.

I get out,
and abandon the car again.
Why let that big beautiful yellow clamp go to waste?
Sure ain't my parking paid for the day?
And so what if I've got nothin' to do?
I've got cigarettes to slay.

Niamh Moroney, a day in the life: Breakfast. Shower. Book circus acts. Lunch. Bus. Teach English or Theatre. Tram. Facilitate a meeting of the BWC if it's Tuesday. Stand on stage and tell jokes if it's Wednesday. See some theatre or attend a rave every other day of the week. This girl is educated, that's all you need to know.

Roumiana Karapetrova
BREATH

I take deep breaths to draw your presence in.
Then slowly sigh your absence out.
I've learned to live with both.

BEGGAR

I wait for you to drop a coin

in my heart a beggar's bowl.

To hear it sing for one brief moment.

CHOICES

I never chose to write of Love.
My choice was Love itself.
But all too eager, I suppose,
I broke my Love with words.

Roumiana Karapetrova graduated with a degree in English Language and Literature from Sofia University. With the political changes in 1989, she took up freelancing. The Chinese curse, "May you live in interesting times!" was in full swing and she was an active participant. Writing poetry was her way out of the box as a staff member with the European Commission.

Andrea Rees
THE COMMUTE

Thank God it's Friday. My hands and wrists ache as I slide my coin into the fare box and listen to the jangle as the gold loonie bounces off the sides and eventually lands flat and inert at the bottom – Queen Elizabeth rather than the loon facing up.

"Transfer please," I say to the driver. If my father isn't there, and he probably won't be, I'll need it later to take the connecting bus home.

The driver smiles at me, his chubby cheeks protruding from his round face. His ugly orange uniform making him look jaundiced. "Thanks," I say, and take the flimsy white strip he's handing to me. It crinkles as I slip it into the front pocket of my jeans.

I make my way into the bus. It starts to rain. The windows become wet, streaky, and only vaguely now can I make out the steel and glass of the shopping centre and the diamond shaped *Square One Mississauga* sign. For a Friday afternoon at 5:15, the bus is pretty empty, but I recognize a girl from the office. I think she's just a couple of years older than me, maybe twenty-one. With her blonde hair and pale skin, many people have told me we could be sisters, but she doesn't talk to me, doesn't even acknowledge me, just like now as I pass her by. I do data entry, the lowest of the low positions. She's a dispatcher. I'm temporary, working for the summer, leaving for university in the fall. She's permanent, not going anywhere, ever.

I slide into an empty, forward-facing two-seater and position myself next to the window. I rest my small bag and my folded, blue and white checked umbrella on my lap. Closer to the front of the bus, a little girl in a flowery dress, one with lots of ribbons and bows, giggles as her mother lifts her into the sideways-facing seat next to her. The girl climbs onto her knees and tries to look out the window, into the grey light. She places a hand on her mother's shoulder. I can't recall ever taking the bus with my own mother, but I think I must have.

A few minutes pass, more people get on, but still it's not very crowded. Finally, the bus revs like a roaring lion, and we pull out of the terminal. We take the road that skirts the mall and then enter the highway. My stomach growls.

I look out the window but can't see much. It's raining harder. Or maybe it just seems like that because we're moving? With my fists, I wipe my eyes to keep them open. We stop and pick up more passengers. Among the group of people, there's another little girl holding her mother's hand. She's carrying ballet shoes. On her way to dance lessons I guess. She looks happy. Her mother looks happy too.

We drive further and then stop once more. This time, a flock of students board. We merge back into traffic and before long we're pulling over yet again. A sole man gets on and he takes the seat, one of the few free ones left, next to me. He's very short, shorter than me. His hair is also short, and curly. But not with tight curls like an Afro, looser and very greasy. His skin is beautiful, a golden brown. He reminds me of our neighbor Jorge.

I try looking out the window again. This time all I can see are abstract shapes and blurs of green, blue, red. Reality distorted by a storm. The bus picks up speed. The ride is now smooth and I rest for a few seconds but suddenly my eyelids pop back open.

Something is pressing, with some force, into my side. I look down. The guy next to me has crossed his arms and it's his elbow I feel. He mustn't realize, I think, and look up into his face. I expect he'll notice my stare, grasp the situation, move his arm, and apologize. But he doesn't. Like with my colleague from the office, I know he knows I'm looking at him, and he does nothing. He continues looking straight ahead, and it's only now that I see his eyes are dark and hard and his mouth is weary and drooped.

I look around wondering, and then hoping that someone has noticed. The little girl in the flowery dress is now sleeping contentedly, her head in her mother's lap, her mother's hand caressing the chestnut tresses that have spilled about. The students are chatting, laughing, and poking fun at each other. One of them presses a button on the cassette player attached to his belt and the blue jay on his baseball cap starts bobbing back and forth. Everyone has a world of their own. My heart starts beating so hard I can hear it in my head. Words rise up in my throat. I don't know you. Stop touching me. You're hurting me. I open my mouth to speak, but nothing comes out.

I try again to say the words, but again I can't. And then, to my surprise, I see safety. I see there is still some space between the window and me and I slide across, moving the gap, placing it between him and me. Problem solved, I think. My frantic heart calms and I rest for a few seconds but then it's pounding uncontrollably again. Once more, I feel his elbow in me, but with more force than before. It's as if he wants to punish me for trying to leave him.

Why are you doing this to me? You're hurting me. But although I try, my voice still fails me. When I need it most, it always fails me. I glare at him, but he doesn't even give me a glance. Again, I look around to discover that no one has noticed. But why would they? And again, I try to speak, but I'm too afraid. Although not of him, really, but of them - of making myself the centre of attention, of no one caring, of no one believing me, of no one wanting to help.

Tears fill my eyes. What do I do? What can I do? And I remember. I remember the folded, checked blue and white umbrella on my lap, and I pick it up and poke it into his paunch with roughly the same force I think he is exerting on me. His fat gives way. His body flinches. His eyes soften. But still he doesn't look at me, and suddenly, I feel a sharper pain in my side. It shoots up into my ribs and takes my breath away. He's pushing even harder. Determined, I push back. We stay like this for a few minutes, until his elbow eases up, but only slightly, followed by my umbrella.

And so we sit for the rest of the journey, side-by-side, facing straight ahead, his elbow prodding into me, my umbrella into him. As the bus exits the highway, heaving and swaying, we are still joined by a secret. Complicit in pain. Connected by pain.

When finally we reach the bus terminal in the expansive parking lot around Shopper's World Brampton, everyone stands up to disembark, but he and I stay seated. He doesn't let go. I don't either. I'm shocked to realize, I don't want to let go.

The sickly-faced bus driver looks into his rearview mirror, sees us, and yells, "End of the line. You have to get off." As if we are one, we both hesitate and then, simultaneously stand up and join the last of the crowd, his arms now free and dangling at his sides and my umbrella from my fingers. I'm just behind him, and he's right behind the girl from my office. From the back, with her short, spiky cut, she could be a man. We file off the bus and I notice that my side still aches even though it's empty. And suddenly I know, it aches because it's empty.

I quickly take a few steps past him, towards the parking lot, and scan the vehicles looking for my father's brown van. Of course he isn't here. The little girl in the flowery dress lets go of her mother's hand and scampers off, and I look back. I see him. He is farther away than I expected but I can still see he is watching and his face is sad. And at that moment, I recognize something of my father, my divorced father. I recognize the face of a man who was abandoned by love.

TRUE LOVE

I look at you, at your dark boldness that makes me tremble, at your sweet smile that steals my breath, and I know I love you and I know I shouldn't, but I can't help myself.

I look at you, at your fingers that are solid and alive and lace perfectly with mine, and I know I love you and I know you're not right for me, but I can't help myself.

I look at you, at your shining, shifting eyes, and I know you don't love me, but I wish you would, because I can't help myself.

Originally from Canada, **Andrea Rees** has lived in Brussels for over a decade. She is passionate about encouraging emotional honesty and reflection, and exploring the intricacy of human relationships and how we connect. Currently, she is finalizing a novel, and an art project, which blends ceramics and words. Her short story *For Jorge* appears in *The Circle*, 2018. Instagram: @_andrea_rees_

Zoheb Mashiur
BRAND NEW ME

All officers, warrant officers, and enlisted men will be provided with a copy of their own true loves that they will never see again, and all these copies will be returnable through the proper channels.

Ernest Hemingway, *Second Poem to Mary*

When I left The Fleet, I had to give-up my accoutrements before re-joining civilian life.

As per standard regulations, Their Majesty's Royal Navy reclaimed the following items:

- 507 Pattern Personal Defence Module, 1 unit
- Combat fatigues, 3 sets
- Junior Officer's dress uniform, 1 suit
- 22 Pattern Junior Officer's Ceremonial Cutlass, 1 unit
- Junior Officer's toiletries, 1 module (partially depleted)
- Naval Officer's Combat Primer, 1 license
- Lover, 1 unit.

The Reclamation Board took away these tokens of a thousand years spent in service, to dispose of at their discretion. Bar the 507, all personal effects were purchasable as keepsakes by retiring servicemen. When I had made the decision to return the fleet's property, it was not because of a lack of money. The package was not cheap, however, I had earned more than enough over the centuries to make it work. Instead, I put my money toward purchasing an estate on Meghla Five.

I fancied the gentleman farmer's life. I saw myself coasting gently above fields of local grasses aboard a vintage needle-ship, sipping sunset wine produced from my own orchards in the shadow of the mountains. I would breed Earth horses, buy a library and read ancient classics in the evenings. I'd marry a true woman and raise the children of my love. These were romantic – and expensive – ambitions. I would have little left to spend on nostalgia.

Suicide, even when done calmly and rationally, is never free of trauma. When I signed my discharge papers, I killed the only self I had known for the past millennium. Just as I had killed my previous self, when I joined the Service. Self-annihilation is ever the first step to self-advancement.

My body was renewed in the Shaping Baths to an approximation of how I was before the wear-and-tear of a thousand years of duty. I hardly recognized my reflection in the mirror: spine compact once more, eyes no longer bloodshot. I ran my finger along my old but new jaw, far squarer than I remembered it being. My grin was perfect; teeth lacking the crookedness of the boy who had joined the Navy all those ages ago. It was me, but not as I had ever been before. The loan of my life repaid by The Service, with interest.

The sun was setting when I stepped out of the Fleet Base at Telamon. Green skies turning sharply violet as nightly rain clouds gathered on the horizon. I had a full night of drinking ahead of me, perhaps in the company of some ladies whose real hearts beat with real warmth.

There was no rush. I realized that I no longer needed to make the most of my time. There was no rush. Never again any rush. No more officers to report back to, no more rationed shore leave. I was ready to live my life accountable only to myself. My brand new self.

Back at Base, my erstwhile lover was surely being tagged for the scrapheap. At the time I felt slight regret. Sentiment had worn thin over the centuries, replaced with jaded familiarity.

I left Telamon after a week's indulgent stay at a hotel. Freedom and the flesh were each as delightful as I'd expected, but the novelty quickly faded. At least I had enough sobriety to call and confirm with the estate agent on Meghla Five that I was available and willing to buy.

I flew economy class, on a slow line. That was a bad year, with poor food and poor company on the ferry ship. I had forgotten how claustrophobic I found extended interaction with civilians; a few hours or days a year trawling through brothels and bars had not demanded much conversation from me. I almost wished I had a shore leave wristwatch counting the hours until I was back in the exclusive company of my peers.

Things took a turn for the better when I arrived at Meghla Five. How to describe that world of clouds? The ferry ship landed with the dawn, glorious yellow sunlight parting the mists like a shimmering curtain. The air was damp but cool when my feet touched solid ground once more, and I felt like singing.

I did sing. Many joined me in the tune, though few knew the words to the old space shanty.

My estate agent sent a needle-ship to meet me at the port. We sailed over the little villages, seas of alveoli grass and rocky streams that were my new home world. Tall forests clung lovingly to mountain faces, vaguely visible through the cloud-walls. My estate was a sprawl of low buildings midst pillars of yellow stone that like pale fingers poking through the mist-shrouded lawn and elevated in rocky levels to great buttes covered in trees yet unclassified. And beyond that, the mountains proper, like the blue rim of a bowl.

It was all I had imagined it to be, but even on the first day it felt curiously empty. It was not a home meant for a single man. The servos and management subroutines were efficient and self-maintaining but no previous owner had bothered with the expense of shipping personality modules all the way to this remote agri-world. For the first time since Telamon, I missed my lover's company.

It would be a lonely existence unless I took steps.

I began to learn something of the ways of the Meghla Five gentry. Most families were related through a cat's cradle of marriage, lazy and fat off the wealth from the local alveoli grass. Fortunes had thinned once cheaper synthetic solutions were found for military red and royal purple dyes, the gentry saddled with estates and lifestyles they could little afford. Fresh blood and treasure were at a premium on the marriage market. A handsome, retiring officer buying up an entire estate, and a millennial officer to boot, caused quite a stir. A thousand years' duty, away from the company of real women, such loneliness and so much pent-up wealth. The locals considered me the most eligible bachelor in the area, as well as one of the easiest. Why, surely, I would fall for the first pretty young thing to bat her eyelashes at me?

The ladies of Meghla Five organized themselves for a serious battle to win my bed and my name for their daughters. I was invited to every dinner, ball and birthday. The girls, in turn, did more than bat their eyelashes through a series of tasteful indiscretions no doubt strategized by their mothers. A little touch of "Oh, Lieutenant, Mama asked if she could possibly borrow that book from your library, and I happened to be passing", and a dash of "Lieutenant, so sorry to call you like this, my needle-ship seems to have jammed, the useless thing. I'm quite close to your estate, could you possibly come…?"

I took what was offered, but lust, I realized, was easily slaked. Love is rarely found. I had already had more than one life's share of love, once in truth and once through artifice, and had walked away on both occasions. Yet I had lived far, far longer than a simple span of the mortal coil. Did all those added centuries of service entitle me to more, or was a life a life no matter its length?

I tried to remember why I'd fallen for her, but whatever it was I couldn't find even a whisper of it in the girls. I found I could not relate to them, their pleasures, and their idle worries. In my head there were a thousand years' worth of memories, joys and mistakes. How could a seventeen-year-old country lass, no matter how grave or sweet she may be, hope to understand me?

Two years passed. It became obvious to my neighbors that my dalliances with their daughters would lead nowhere. Consequently, I became less welcome as a dinner guest, and my home became a forbidden place. A few girls, who had taken an honest shine to me, still arranged rendezvous, but I did not wish to invite quarrel with their fathers. I turned them down.

As I shooed one twenty-two-year-old away from my porch, she asked, "Lieutenant, do you know why girls desire you?"

"No. Please, it is not appropriate for you to be h–"

"I daresay many of the things you asked me to do in this house weren't appropriate either. You probably think we wanted your money, but only our parents cared about that. We just wanted someone who'd seen things we hadn't." Her smile was bitter. "I used to dream you would tell me about beautiful stars, distant worlds, and strange histories after making love. I'd hold you close, and listen. Silly dreams.

"Instead, Lieutenant, every time you finished with me, you would go lie in your bath and light your pipe. You made me feel like something that had to be washed off. A strange lesson for a girl."

She began to walk to her horse. I saw her riding dress was backless, and remembered how that part of her felt under my fingers. "So why return to me?"

She shrugged on horseback, "Even if you never gave me what I really wanted, what you did give, you gave well. I missed that at the very least."

"You are too young to know what you want," I tried to explain, patiently.

"I know I am." Her smile widened like the void outside a porthole. Beautiful. Cold. "But what's your excuse?"

By the time I had a response to that, she had left. But then, what chance would an old man such as I have had against the certainty of youth?

Life on Meghla Five lost its lustre. The golden clouds of dawn never failed to rouse my finer feelings, but at other times the land seemed strange, eerie, and oppressive. During walks between the yellow rocks in my parks, I felt alone, walking a grey world that existed only around me and the ground just under my feet. Even the distant forests on their vast columns of stone were blotted out, and all I saw were the rocky fingers rising before my eyes like yellow ghosts in the fog. All creation itself seemed to conspire to reject and isolate me.

I bought the library. I read the books, but the stories of love and friendship made my situation stand out ever clearer in contrast. I took no pleasure in them, and lost all interest in the acres of my estate. The needle-ship languished in its hangar, and as for the horses, I never got around to buying them.

One evening, I received a call from a society hostess who lived across the mountain range from me. Relations between us had cooled since she had found a more pliable match for her daughter, but she was all charm and grace.

"Lieutenant," she began, her voice fashionably sing-song. "However do you do? It really has been too long."

"I am well, Madame. I trust you and your family are in good health."

"Ah, but we are marvellous. Thank you so much for asking. It has been such a while since my husband and I last had the pleasure of your company. I wonder, might you care to join us for dinner tomorrow? I hope it's not an imposition on your time."

She, of course, knew very well that nothing ever imposed on my time. "I would be honoured, Madame. Is there any special occasion?"

"No, no, not as such. Just a small gathering of friends and neighbours. In fact, you should be there especially, because we do have a guest of honour of sorts. Would you happen to know a Lieutenant Monocher?"

"I cannot say that I do, Madame."

"Ah, how marvelously odd! Like you, he has retired from Their Majesty's Navy. He bought Peaktop Farm just last week. Imagine that: two officers retiring to our humble little world, and both such close neighbours! You simply must meet him, I'm sure you would have so much to talk about!"

I was being invited only to bridge the conversation gap between the Meghla Five estate-owners and Lieutenant Monocher. Very well, I could consent to an evening of being used; I was myself curious to meet my brother officer. I accepted the invitation with thanks.

Monocher turned out to be a fairly reserved man who stood on ceremony. He would have no struggle adjusting to life outside The Service because in his head he'd never really left. We made a stark contrast at our hostess' home: I wearing the same local formals as the other guests, and Monocher in his junior officers' dress uniform. He of course would have considered it madness not to take the keepsakes of his career with him, and I saw a little disappointment in his eyes at seeing me so blatantly civilian.

Our conversation at the dinner table was none of the best, but we made appointments to visit each other's estates soon. I looked forward to spending more time with someone who had known the same life, even if he was otherwise priggish.

The flight up the cloud cover to Monocher's home was the first exhilarating experience I had had that year. Peaktop Farm was much smaller than my estate but, perched on a yellow-stone butte, it commanded a grand view over the countryside for many a league. From that spot, the distance between neighbours seemed much shorter.

Monocher's robots brought us tea while we chatted on the observation deck. We traded war stories and anecdotes about life on the Fleet: his recent enough to count as gossip. I felt that he was relaxing in my company. He was much less uptight out of uniform anyway. After a while, I even grew bold enough to tell him so.

I was pleased to see him looking sheepish. He apologized and said that a lifetime of habits was not so easily discarded. He would embrace the facts of his retirement, but ever so slowly. "In fact," he said, "I admire the ease with which you have transitioned, Lieutenant."

"I found it easiest at the very start. I committed myself to making a total break from my old life; I tried to think of it as suicide."

"Is that why you refused the keepsakes of the Service?" he asked.

"Yes."

"Hmm. I admit that they act as a sort of… armour, protecting me from the realities of being Lieutenant Monocher, Royal Navy, retired. Perhaps I should think about parting ways with a few of my effects. Do you think that might help, Lieutenant?"

"It is worth trying."

Lunch consisted of local ingredients cooked down to military levels of quality. It alone was certain proof that Monocher's nostalgia for the Service was not doing him any good. After dinner there was coffee – quite good coffee. I asked about his plans for the future.

"I am unsure. I suppose I am 'settling down' as they say. I might find a pretty country girl. Our hostess intimated that there were many options for eligible bachelors such as ourselves."

"I dare say, in no time at all you will be up to your collar in offers to marry the local offspring."

"I'm surprised that the matrons did not get their hooks in you, Lieutenant. If I may say so, it is difficult for a Navy man to live utterly without the company of a woman. Our habits die hard."

"Well, being unmarried does not make me a monk. Though, I will caution you, a married man would have an easier social life here."

"I understand you, I think." He blushed, slightly. "I fully intend to marry, but in the meantime, my needs are taken care of."

I raised my eyebrows. "You already have an understanding with a woman here?"

"Not as such. I am not very good with women. I did however keep more from my career than a few suits to wear to dinner."

"I see." I paused. "And she is here?"

"She is." He smiled, his face was made even more handsome with the pleasure he took from acknowledging her.

"The real one must have been an exceptional woman," I ventured, a strange, unaccountable jealousy in my heart.

He frowned. "I suppose so…but I hardly remember. It is strange… I hadn't thought of it before." Monocher looked at me, suddenly puzzled. "I can't remember her at all."

There was a pause as he looked at his coffee, brows furrowed as though seeking some revelation in murk as muddy as his memory.

"May I meet her?" I blushed as soon as the words slipped out, the colour of my skin hiding it. I do not know why I asked – in the Fleet, we never saw another officer's lover. It was simply not done, not even by the boors who boasted of their encounters with women on shore leave.

Naturally, Monocher looked shocked at my request, but slowly relaxed.

"Well… why not? A new life, no need to stand on the old ceremonies, yes?" He smiled, uncertain, but willing to try change.

I self-consciously tidied myself as Monocher called for her using his wrist display. A silly thing to do, grooming myself for a mere duplicate, but I couldn't help it. After so many years, to see another of her kind again… I had dreamt of her face almost every night since I had left her at Telamon base to be decommissioned. The same face I had left back on Earth a thousand years earlier. Of course, Monocher's lover would have a different face, the face of the one he desired.

But it might resemble hers. If so, it was the closest I would get to her again.

She came into the dining room wearing a light blue knee-length dress that hung from simple straps on her shoulders. Her gait was familiar, her shape and posture evoking memories they should not have. In fact, all of her was heart-stopping familiar.

"Hello, Lieutenant." That voice…sharp as a bird's.

I stuttered in disbelief.

Monocher looked alarmed. I seemed to hear his voice from the bottom of a well. "What's wrong? Lieutenant? Speak to me, man! What is –?"

My lover. My love. Hers was the face he looked at when he fucked.

"Is this… is this who you have always been with?" I asked, slowly, my mind racing. Was mine not scrapped at Telamon after all? Reassigned to him by some fluke or–?

"Yes! Yes, damn it, man! Why are you asking?" He looked at his – my – our lover.

"Describe her," I said. Had we loved the same woman, once upon a time? What madness was this? Jealousy trembled within me.

"What?"

I slammed my fist on the table, coffee mugs scattering, spilling onto my trousers. My lover jumped. "Describe her!"

"My God, Lieutenant, control yourself…!" He raised his hands, then slowly lowered them, concern etched across his maddeningly perfect face. "But alright… I'll humour you. She's tall."

She was not.

"Thin and graceful like a willow."

She was small as a doll. Quite voluptuous.

"Long flowing locks to her waist, raven-black…"

It was straight and honey-blonde, shoulder-length with fringe. "Go on," I breathed, my temples throbbing. "Her face. Tell me about her face."

He shook his head. "What are you playing at, man? But… fine. Full, rosy cheeks, dimpled chin, uh, freckles across a small nose, green eyes –"

"No, no, no, no…" I grabbed his hand. "I don't see that! Not a word of that!"

"What? How could you not?"

"Please, Lieutenant, calm down," our lover murmured, and I wondered if he heard her voice as deep and husky, perhaps sharing his accent. She reached out her hand to me, and I saw the little scar on her forearm I used to kiss.

A copy, we were told. Designed to evoke a memory. A copy of whom?

Copies of each other, and our longing hearts shaped our copies into what we wished to see. No wonder we never saw each other's women while in the Service. How could we bear to see our lovers in another's arms, even if he saw her as his? It was all to avoid the jealous, black rage that was trembling through my body.

"Speak to me, Lieutenant!" Monocher cried, as I turned to flee. It was not his fault. I had asked to see her, and as a result I learned what was not for me to know. But I knew I would hate Monocher forever. He had her now. I paused before boarding my needle-ship for one final look into those familiar brown eyes.

She did not know me.

Zoheb Mashiur stumbled into academia and is now far too involved to back out. He completed his MA at the University of Kent's Brussels School of International Studies in 2019, and is currently an Early Stage Researcher at Charles University, Prague. In 2017, Zoheb edited the anthology *Disconnect: Collected Short Fiction* (Borshadupur), showcasing the work of young Bangladeshi newcomers.

Jay Harold
ROSABELLE AVENUE

A packet of smokes, one whiskey to go,
walking down Rosabelle Avenue.
Footsteps so heavy, I nearly broke the levee
After that girl twice played me for a fool.

I'm on the run, just about done
with not knowing what I'm supposed to do.
Sick of regretting what I'm not getting,
walking down Rosabelle Avenue.

When the memories rush back and
I try to slip away.
Rosabelle Avenue, ain't much light left to you
but I know I'll see you again one day.

WIVENHOE DREAMING

In my Wivenhoe dream I see the moon
at high noon, thinking life wasn't so bad
Letting some light in
from celestial bodies and three AM writing…

Back to smokin' and smog, far from Wivenhoe Town,
and those six-string sets at the Rose and Crown.
I'm fading in my room, tangentially,
just a shadow of the poet that I used to be.

When the Good Lord greets me in the endgame,
I'll pray to go to Wiv' again,
and wash away with Mersea's tide,
put the top down for one last ride.

But to reminisce is a foolish man's game,
Should I return, things would never be the same.
Yes! I know, though sad as it may seem,
I will never say no to a Wivenhoe dream

Jay Harold holds a masters' degree in Creative Writing from the University of Essex and is a member and a former chair of the Brussels Writers' Circle. He is currently working in Amsterdam as an editorial assistant.

Irina Papancheva
SAUDADE

"You've got the best pastels de nata in town. As I eat them, I close my eyes and see myself again in Lisbon. Sitting on the stairs, descending to the delta."

She closed her eyes while saying this, her face turned slightly upward and her neck stretched as if expecting to be kissed. I wished I had my camera with me. Her eyes opened slightly and she gave me a misty-eyed look as if she was emerging from a beautiful dream.

"You've been there many times?" I ask.

"I did my masters there, long ago, now. Then, I kept returning. Part of my soul is there and keeps calling me back."

Her Portuguese was flowing easily with its own charming melody, coloured by her Italian accent.

"Perhaps we could have a Portuguese dinner sometime and share our memories."

"Perhaps we could." Her dark eyes sparkled.

She walked away with a paper bag full of pastels de nata, leaving her business card in my hand and me swirling from the encounter and its possible continuation.

That's the beauty of working at such a place. You meet all sorts of people, and occasionally, some attractive people. Mostly friendly people, Portuguese or having some connection to Portugal, like this woman. Our pastels are the taste of home far away from home.

Fifteen years ago, when my cousin Pedro called to suggest that I join him in this venture, I didn't hesitate. I was stuck in a troubled marriage and had already realised that photography would not make me rich. It took a couple of days of thinking about the *how*. The *if* was sorted out.

A visit to my mother, who dropped a couple of tears. Fresh flowers for my dad, who blessed me from his grave. An evening out with Jose and Luis who kept topping up my glass with wine on the background of fado.

And adiós.

My wife Luisa kept her lips tight and her eyes shone wet as I was leaving that morning, but I know her tears were from anger, not sadness. Anger that it was me who was managing to escape from our dysfunctional existence, not her.

I left Portugal only to find another Portugal here. From Saint Gilles, through Ixelles to Etterbeek, reminders of my country surround me. Portuguese shops, cafes, restaurants; each one a small island offering shelter to my compatriots' longing after what we have left behind. And even if this is an illusion, a mere imitation, Pedro and I seized the opportunity and joined the team of those trying to keep it alive. Pastels de nata; a taste of home.

Even Fernando Pessoa has found a home here, at Flagey. I visit him every so often for a silent conversation, while having a smoke, standing the test of his eyes behind the stone glasses. This time, it goes like this:

Fernando: "The feelings that hurt most, the emotions that sting are those that are absurd; the longing for impossible things, precisely because they are impossible…"

Me: "Tell me about it, man. That's the story of my life…"

"…nostalgia for what never was; the desire for what could have been; regret over not being someone else; dissatisfaction with the world's existence."

"Indeed. The tireless hope, that perhaps this time…"

"All these half-tones of the soul's consciousness create in us a painful landscape, an eternal sunset of what we are."

That's the problem of communicating through the ether – the greats don't listen, do they? They just pour their wisdom over you; get it or not, you've got to move on with your little life, get lost in your own painful landscape, kill the monster, hold the thread, which will take you out of it, so that you most probably commit your next betrayal and find yourself in a landscape which looks different but is even more painful than the last til you realize that there is no exit. Just standing in front of Pessoa's statue makes me a philosopher. The one book I took with me when leaving Portugal was his *Book of Disquiet*.

As the eternal sunset colours the sky over Brussels, I finish a beer in Maison de Peuple and recall the dusk in Elisa's eyes. I send her a message: 'How about having that dinner tomorrow?'

Two minutes later, my phone beeps. 'With pleasure', but the message is not from Elisa. It's from Iris.

"Damn it," I'd already written her off; she'd taken too long to reply. We'd met three days ago on tinder and ventured out on an immediate date in Hortense, the bar I prefer for setting the scene. She was attractive and smart, and, perhaps, a bit lonely. It was an interesting rendezvous and warranted a follow-up. I invited her for dinner at my place. She had been silent ever since. I laughed at myself. What are the odds? If Elisa accepts, I could cook for both; a special Portuguese dinner with desert served in my king size bed... But Elisa fast extinguishes my boyish fantasies: 'Tomorrow, not possible. How about Friday?'

The following evening, I welcome Iris to my flat, just around the corner from Parvis de Saint Gilles. She wears a blue dress. Dark, with short sleeves and a hint of glitter. It suits her. Her wavy hair falls freely across her back in a way that makes me want to caress it. I don't. Impatience is the biggest enemy of being strategic. And, without sounding cynical, that's what I have learnt to be with women.

Not like a lobbyist, following only my own interests. No. Romance is about allowing the woman to take her time, to relax, to breathe, to feel the space around her and the space between you while you plant the seeds of desire and begin cultivating them. That's the beauty of it. That's what makes each date unique and exciting. The different sense of space for every woman; her own timing. It's like in photography. You would never get a good portrait by telling the model what to do, how to turn, where to look. This results in cold images of living statues. Soulless. Give your model the freedom to explore, move and search, connect to you and to the camera. That's when amazing things can happen. Art can happen. And in relationships, it's the connection that happens. The art of seduction is slow dancing in one rhythm.

Iris eats the fish I have cooked and drinks the white wine I have chosen for her, then looks at me with anticipation. A mixture of suspicion and curiosity; her writer's soul peeping through.

"Fernando Pessoa said, that to write is to forget and that literature is the most agreeable way of ignoring life. Literature retreats from life by turning into slumber, but then, it also simulates life."

I throw the subject of literature on the table like dice, hoping to get the lucky number.

"He must be right. Interestingly, I produced a similar thought in a short story after our date."

"I'd love to read your story, perhaps one day."

She eats slowly, sipping wine after every bite in small measured sips. The fork and the knife rest on her plate as she chews.

"Cheers to our freedom. The end of the lockdown!" I mock.

"As if this changes anything… cheers," she smiles, then drinks.

"Of course, it doesn't. Today makes no difference from yesterday, and yesterday makes no difference from all the preceding days."

"I am not entirely sure about that. People being killed in cafes, museums and concert halls in Europe isn't something that happens every day. But you're right that the lockdown was exaggerated, and that the security presence means nothing. I don't feel any safer today because I know this could happen at any time, despite the troops and their tanks."

By the time we take dessert, I know as much about her as when she entered my apartment. I wonder whether being mysterious is her fashion or her true self? I imagined her talking about the books she has written and the books she has read, drowning me in an ocean of intellectualism, spiritualism and many other-isms. But she's not trying to impress me. She's just sitting here, eating the food, sipping the wine and listening to me. And as she is so silent, I feel obliged to do all the talking. Lisbon, Brussels, Pessoa, photography… I talk, she listens. Only when she tastes my pastels de nata, does her expression change.

"You made these?"

I think I finally managed to impress her.

Afterwards she goes to my photo wall. Some of my best shots, along with favourite photographs by others, hang there. I join her.

"My wall of fame."

She smiles and looks at me. Suddenly it's easy to raise my hand and caress her hair. I make a short step forward and kiss her. She responds in the same knowing manner. There is a special quality to it, which I'm trying to name. Purity. That's what it is. Somehow, the way she kisses is both experienced and tantalizingly chaste. She says, "It's getting late. I'll call a taxi."

It's only eleven.

I walk her down stairs and kiss her again. As her taxi departs, I head to Bar du Matin. People are standing in front, talking and smoking. Inside, it's busy. An Afro-American band is performing something full of rhythm and sun. I order a beer at the bar and look around. A mixed crowd, as usual, laid back. Artists, students, NGO workers, the job-less, newly single. The beer goes down nicely.

Two women come up next to me and order drinks.

"Bourbon," says the one closest.

"Cheers," I say, once she's holding the glass of golden liquid.

"Cheers," she smiles, and then follows her friend to a table. Blond hair, not very long, slender body, she sits opposite me and our eyes meet. I could get up, go to them and ask to join, then sit close to her, discover the scent of her hair and perfume, talk in her ear, give myself over to the night and its unpredictability. I could. And that's what matters, the potential of it. I finish my beer, throw her one last look, nod in her direction and walk to the door.

In bed I send a message to Iris: 'It was lovely. Let's do it again soon. Sweet dreams.'

There are two types of light that make for good street pictures: the earliest morning light, and the very nearly evening light. The silver of the awakening, and the gold of the fading day. I never get tired of trying to capture the light as it hits the features of the city. Cities are living beings, organisms, each a micro-universe functioning with perfect simplicity. Their features change every day, reflecting time and happenings.

In the days, weeks and months following the so-called lockdown, armed men in public spaces become a permanent feature. My camera avoids them as much as possible. There have been enough of these photos. However, one early morning, as I pass by the Haitian embassy, something unusual happens; the features change. A young woman with an angelic face approaches one of the soldiers in front of the Embassy and gives him a box of chocolates. She looks into his eyes, says something, and then leaves. There is grace in how she walks away without looking back.

The soldier holds the box with an astonished expression. Then a smile brightens his face, making it look completely different – gentle, human. Miraculously, I've captured the moment when she gives him the box and they look into each other's eyes. It is easily my best and most acclaimed photo.

Equipped with my camera, I'm not a lone walker. I'm an observer. A moment catcher. An unconventional beauty discoverer.

The Parvis de Saint Gilles is a great spot for portraits and street shots. The crowded cafes, the drinks and food trucks with people standing around eating and drinking, the passersby, the markets on Thursday nights and at the weekend. This is where I make my 'Free Brussels' series. I include a photo of the prison building as a reminder that everyone on the outside is free to live their life. What fascinates me is that at social gatherings nobody talks about what has happened. As if ignoring it makes it non-existent. Freedom means forgetting the past and not fearing the future.

On Friday evening I am having a caipirinha in Coimbra, waiting for Elisa. The tables around me are occupied. It's mostly my compatriots. Luisa and I spent a weekend in Coimbra once upon a time, in another life, when we were still in love. We walked around the river late one summer evening holding hands marveling at the golden reflections of light in the indigo water. We stopped and kissed under a tree, and that kiss, that night, the tenderness and excitement it contained felt like a silent promise for eternity.

"Olá!"

Elisa has arrived with her wild, dark hair, disarming smile and misty eyes. I get up and give her a hug, one peck on each cheek. The strong, sweet smell of her perfume makes me dizzy. She's wearing black skinny jeans, high heel boots and an orange top revealing a tiny bit of her lacy black bra. Just looking at her creates that familiar tension that I feel needs to be released as a matter of urgency. Self-control man. Breathing in, breathing out. Going through all the pleasantries and savouring every course, each with its own drink. And as we laugh and talk, the only thing I can think of is making love to her.

Later that night all the unspoken promises are fulfilled. In the darkness of my bedroom, with Elisa, I experience the most exhilarating state of freedom.

Friday, the week after, I walk through a dark open space at the bottom in Rue Cellule, not far away from Bar du Matin. I haven't seen Iris since our dinner. I send her a message, 'When can I see you?' to which she replies, 'I'll be at a Milonga in Saint Gilles after 10 pm tonight. Come and join me.'

I take the stairs up. The corridor has a clothes hanger and a pile of shoes all around it. A young woman sits at a small table just beyond the entrance. I pay the entrance fee.

Couples move on the dance floor in a coordinated manner, as if this is a choreographed scene from a film. There are chairs and small tables next to the wall, the light is muted. People hang around the bar, chatting and throwing looks at the dancing couples. I go to the bar and order a small whiskey, stealing glances at the dancers. Iris is there, dancing with a taller man, in a very close embrace. Their cheeks touch; her eyes are closed. Her hair is gathered at the nape of her neck. She's wearing a black dress with thin straps that wraps her body, and red shoes with very high heels. Her movements are smooth, sensual, she seems to be enjoying every single stretch. Nothing is rushed. Then, one fast kick in the air and she's back to her serene flow.

The harmony between her and the man is striking, their movements completing each other. I reach for my camera, bump up the ISO, and take a few close shots. I capture the expressions on their faces. Their legs. Their hands.

"It's the heart that matters in tango. All the rest, it only manifests their connection. That's why the leading comes from the chest," Iris tells me later as we sit at a small table, slightly off the dance floor. I gently massage her fingers; her hands are cool. We look at the other couples and don't talk much. It's peaceful. Rather different from the experience I had with Elisa. The thing is, I need both. The mysterious and serene air of Iris; the voluptuous presence of Elisa. The problem is: I cannot have both. And making a choice seems rather difficult.

A slow kiss in the street before the cab takes Iris away. As I walk back to my home, I think of the words of my famous compatriot. "The longing for impossible things, precisely because they are impossible; nostalgia for what never was."

That's saudade. The quintessence of my love life.

Irina Papancheva, Bulgarian, is the author of the illustrated children's book *I Stutter* (Ciela, 2005), the novels *Almost Intimately* (Kronos, 2007), *Annabel* (Janet 45, 2010), *Pelican Feather* (Janet 45, 2013), *She, the island* (Trud, 2017) and short stories. Her work has been translated to English, French, Arabic and Persian. *Saudade* is a chapter from her latest manuscript. Website: http://ipapancheva.com/en/

TD Arkenberg
PARVIS DE SAINT-GILLES

Parvis de Saint-Gilles was shortlisted as a finalist in the William Faulkner - William Wisdom Creative Writing Competition

Nigel Escott hurried across the nearly deserted parvis. The lead-colored sky that stalled above the city that September produced an incessant drizzle sufficient to sour the spirits of those with the sunniest of temperaments. Even on his best days, Nigel Escott would never be mistaken for sunny. Not any longer; not after years of dashed hopes and faded dreams.

"Bloody Belgian climate!" he cursed as the paper-thin soles of his loafers sloshed into a puddle.

Nigel's pace quickened over the rain-splattered paving stones. A glance at the clock on the church steeple indicated a few minutes before nine. 'Early enough for my usual table and favorite newspapers', he thought. His hand patted the pocket of his worn blue trousers. No, haven't forgotten my change. He'd scavenged just enough coins from a bureau drawer for two coffees and a croissant. Flicking water from his green safari jacket, he dashed into the Maison du Peuple.

Although the parvis contained many cafes, the Maison du Peuple, or MDP as locals called it, was certainly the most popular. The ambience was more reminiscent of hipster coffeehouses in Amsterdam, New York, and London than the staid, traditional cafes of Paris and Brussels. Young entrepreneurs had bought and transformed the MDP into a trendy hangout. It attracted a mix of artists, writers, journalists, students, and self-employed consultants from Saint-Gilles, one of Brussels' more bohemian municipalities. On weekends, live performers and specialty disc jockeys molded the cafe's brand and grew its customer base. Although the Maison du Peuple had a decidedly youthful tilt at night, the cafe served a broader demographic during the day. Inside, one was likely to hear more than a dozen languages. On market days, the carnival atmosphere of a bustling parvis spilled into the MDP.

As Nigel navigated to the long wooden bar, he scanned the room. Among patrons, many with eyes glued to computer screens, he recognized only a smattering of faces. But it was still early. Gazing at the shelf of foreign-language papers, he was in luck—early enough to snare *The Times of London* and *El Pais*, the Spanish daily. With newspapers in hand, he perched on a barstool and called to the server, "Un cafe et un croissant, s'il vous plait."

After counting out the dozen coins needed to make three euros for the breakfast special, he scanned *The Times*. Although he'd lived on the Continent for nearly three decades and hadn't set foot on British soil in years, he considered England his home. His aged father, nearly ninety-five years old, and two older brothers, with whom Nigel had been estranged for years, still lived in London. He wanted to believe that his father's disdain for his youngest son's undistinguished career and foreign escapades had mellowed with age. As for his brothers, a barrister and a surgeon, he assumed time had only hardened their opinion that Pudgy Nudgy, as they called him, remained an unrepentant dreamer and utter disappointment.

Nigel groaned at the paper's headline warning of cataclysmic deficits plaguing the National Health Service. "Catastrophe," he mumbled. Another article detailed an uptick in activity at the Calais refugee camp dubbed The Jungle. Recent weeks saw a spike in attempts by asylum seekers huddled in the French port to board lorries destined for the United Kingdom. Nigel didn't have an answer to the refugee question, but he was sympathetic to the plight of those fleeing homelands for a better life. His family never forgave him for leaving their blessed plot, this earth, and this realm, their England.

A pouty-faced server slid a cup of creamy coffee and a basket containing a croissant across the bar. Nigel offered a perfunctory "Merci." With raised eyebrow, the server silently scooped the change into his palm and turned to the register. Nigel sighed. The MDP had been his morning ritual since relocating to Brussels three years before. But with rare exception, staff treated him like a stranger. Not that he felt singled out. Staff treated most customers with a cool detachment, reserving collegial banter for coworkers. Nigel wondered whether surliness and sneers were prerequisites for a job, maybe even part of the hipster allure. Or, perhaps, indifference was simply a trait of the younger generation. It hadn't been like that when he was a teenager, forty-odd years before, waiting tables on holidaymakers in Brighton, or so he believed.

Tucking both newspapers under his arm, Nigel grabbed the basket and coffee. Tables at the front of the cafe were his favorites. Windows that reached to the ceiling captured what scant natural light existed in Brussels. On either side of the entrance, long banquettes with tired cushions lined walls of exposed brick. One side featured a colorful mural, a tropical scene of Gauguin-inspired women, palm trees, a volcano, and coffee beans. The cafe's logo, three intertwined initials outlined in purple, graced the opposite wall. In between, simple wooden tables covered an expansive planked floor.

Nigel preferred the banquettes. Others did too. These seats filled first when the cafe opened at half past eight. Nigel's spot of choice, nearest the window and under the tropical mural, was still vacant. After placing his breakfast on the table, he draped his damp coat over the straight-backed chair then slid onto the cushioned bench. Just a matter of time, he thought, before the cafe fills to the brim. He gazed to his immediate right. Regular patrons including Nigel understood implicitly that the empty table was reserved for an elderly couple, native Bruxellois by the looks of them.

As if on cue, the white-haired man and woman, both tall and lean, tottered toward their table. They looked paler and more haggard than usual. Their vacant eyes and long stoic faces repelled greetings and chitchat. From observation, Nigel knew the couple's routine. They drank coffee in silence, side by side on the banquette, their backs to the wall. With chin raised and face devoid of emotion, the woman surveyed the cafe as the man hunched over a Belgian newspaper. They didn't converse with others and communicated with each other only in hushed whispers and nonverbal cues. They lingered only until the man finished the newspaper. After their silent departure, the prime table became fair game.

Two years before, Nigel witnessed a short exchange in French between the couple and an elderly gentleman who wandered into the MDP. Nigel didn't understand what was said, but the woman's eyes sparked to life. Blue they were. She smiled, maybe even blushed. She had been attractive once, maybe even beautiful, he thought at the time. But that was long ago. The arrival of a well-dressed woman, arrogant in manner, who Nigel assumed was the gentleman's wife, extinguished the spark and ended the exchange. That brief encounter was Nigel's sole glimpse into the couple's lives.

A tap on Nigel's table accompanied a familiar voice. "Buongiorno, Signor Escott."

Nigel looked up from his paper and nodded at the man who wore a wrinkled denim shirt and baggy trousers. He considered Renzo an acquaintance as he did most cafe regulars, but nothing more. Noticing a cane, Nigel's eyes dropped to the floor. Renzo's foot was bandaged and set in a therapeutic boot. "What happened to you?"

Renzo, an avid cyclist, explained that a motorist who took the "right-turn priority" rule quite literally plowed his Fiat into him on Avenue Louise. "Good thing the driver wasn't German," Renzo added. "A BMW or Mercedes would have meant curtains. The Fiat fared far worse than this hardy Italian." His deep laugh informed Nigel that the man wasn't terribly hurt.

"We'll talk later," Renzo said, hobbling off to fetch a coffee from the bar before taking his usual seat on the banquette on the other side of the elderly Belgian couple.

Nigel gazed out the window. Beyond the reflection of his unruly hair, puffy dark eyes, and sagging jawline, another acquaintance trekked across the parvis. Before Michael Bergeron stepped into the Maison du Peuple, he shook rain from his cap. Thinning blond hair and a high forehead made him look older than his forty years. Above a weak chin that anchored his narrow face were thin lips and gray eyes set too close together. A large nose was his noblest feature. In the time Nigel had known him, Michael never spoke of a romantic interest, mentioning only a mother in Quebec.

Nigel snickered. Blocking the exit to wipe drizzle from his wire-rimmed glasses, Michael appeared oblivious to the sneer and mumbled curses of a cafe employee on his way outside for a smoke. After dropping his shoulder bag onto an empty table, Michael finally made eye contact with Nigel who offered a friendly nod.

Michael would remain there until the elderly couple completed their morning ritual. Then, he'd relocate to their vacated table between Nigel and Renzo. At that time, the three men shared news, gossip, and adventures. That had been the trio's daily routine for the past three years.

The elderly couple rose slowly from their seats and put on their coats. The woman's deep, hacking cough interrupted their customary silence. She clutched her chest with one hand and steadied her balance with her other hand on the tabletop. Alarm flashed across her companion's face. Recovering, the woman repulsed his advancing arm with an icy glare.

After they left, Nigel looked across the room. Michael folded the Paris newspaper and grabbed his jacket. As he crossed the cafe, to claim his customary spot, a young woman with long blonde hair cut him off. Michael froze, a look of shock on his face. Stirring up a cloud of jasmine-scented perfume, the woman swung her bag onto the banquette between Nigel and Renzo. Without acknowledging either man, she placed a cup of hot tea and a pastry on the empty table. Nigel reckoned she was no more than thirty. Her clothes were urban chic and she had an air of confidence that intrigued him.

Michael remained at a standstill, his expression turning from surprise to annoyance. Nigel stared at the woman. Renzo, he noticed, did the same. She removed a laptop from her bag, oblivious to having disrupted the natural order of things at the Maison du Peuple. Already plotting how to get the pretty young thing into his bed, Nigel feared that Renzo might intercede on Michael's behalf. Whoever speaks first, Nigel thought, will seal the Canadian's fate...and mine.

After smoothing his hair and adjusting his rumpled shirt, Nigel attempted to get the woman's attention by clearing his throat. When that didn't work, he added, "Dreadful weather we're having." A rare smile, tilt of his head, and exaggerated Oxbridge accent were Nigel's signature tactics to charm the opposite sex.

Ignoring Michael's chest-heaving sigh and dramatic pivot to reclaim his former seat, Nigel repeated his climatic observation. This time in a louder, more confident voice.

The young woman shrugged. "I'm used to it. Seattle's home."

Nigel flinched. "American? Hmm, don't get many of your countrymen, or should I say countrywomen, in these parts," he said with a chuckle. "Welcome, welcome. My name's Nigel."

"English," she said more as a statement than a question. Accepting his hand, she introduced herself as Jenny Stein. "I'm a journalist. Here to write a series on refugees."

"Well then, Brussels is the place to be. Bureaucrats will have it all figured out, mark my words."

Jenny laughed. Nigel laughed too.

"That's just it," she said, her tone filling with scorn. "Solutions will come from the front lines. They always do. In-your-face crisis demands action. EU officials should be leading, but they won't." She pointed at Nigel's newspaper. "There, you see. Calais is a mess. Greece is a mess, the Balkans are a mess, and so on."

Renzo's exaggerated cough got Nigel's attention. "Jenny, my apologies. Beside you is Renzo Gatti. Another Brussels wayfarer."

The journalist turned and shook hands with the Italian. "Nice to meet you."

"We're regulars. Michael too," Renzo said, motioning across the cafe. Michael's glare, puckered lips, and furrowed brow suggested that he was still seething. "As a matter of fact, you've taken his spot."

"Oh, I…I didn't know. My apologies. I'll move." Jenny began to shut her laptop.

Catching Jenny's hand, Nigel shot Renzo a nasty look. "There are no reserved seats. You're welcome to sit anywhere. We're all just migrant birds who live around the parvis. We can get a bit too territorial, that's all."

"By the way," Jenny said, slowly extracting her hand from his, "what's a parvis?"

Nigel sat up, puffing out his chest. "An open enclosed space."

Jenny looked at Nigel over her pain au chocolat. "I thought it meant place, as in, Grand Place."

"Ah, yes, common mistake. Parvis refers specifically to an area in front of a church or cathedral. I'm assuming you noticed the church on your way in." Jenny nodded. "Neo-Roman, nineteenth century." Placing her elbow on the table, Jenny rested her chin in her palm. Observing her keen interest, Nigel embellished. "Parvis is derived from paradise. An ancient lineage— Persian, Greek, Latin. Original meaning is an enclosure."

Nigel basked in the journalist's gaze, which he interpreted as respect, admiration, and maybe something more. His chances of bedding the woman, he calculated, had improved markedly. With her back to Renzo, Jenny didn't notice the Italian roll his eyes. With a silent scoff, he returned to the Italian newspaper.

"So, what brings you here—"

"Nigel," he interjected, sensing Jenny struggle to recall his name. "Left England thirty years ago. Pursued a lovely senorita to Barcelona. Marriage soured, followed shortly thereafter by a business or two. Made my way here three years ago. The rest, as they say, is a long story with which I won't bore you. Suffice it to say, Brussels is comparatively inexpensive as European capitals go. Not the best place I've lived; not the worst either."

"I think it's charming, Nigel. History, ancient architecture, interesting people. For a journalist, Brussels is ripe with stories at the moment. I'll grab what I can, then off to Hungary in a few days. Might even be enough material for a book."

Nigel recognized her genuine exuberance. Americans found everything in Europe darling, quaint, charming—even if it was made in China. He didn't object. As a matter of fact, it gave him certain advantages with the ladies. "Yes," he replied. "Brussels has some charm. But it's a bit like Casablanca." The woman's puzzled expression prompted him to add, "You have seen the film?"

"Of course. Bogart and Bergman, two of my favorites. But the connection to Brussels?"

Nigel craned his head around the cafe. Most of the patrons, he surmised, were expats like him. He returned his gaze to Jenny. "We're all waiting for the Lisbon plane."

"Lisbon plane?"

"Most expats I've encountered view Brussels as a way station. All have plans or, at the very least, dreams of moving on. Maybe that's why the Belgians keep to themselves." An image of the just-exited couple popped into his head. "They view the rest of us as transients, or worse, interlopers and opportunists."

Nigel gestured toward the bar. Renzo was ordering another coffee. "Take my handsome friend. Left Italy two decades ago. Fled the seminary. Or was he expelled? Doesn't matter. Considers himself lucky to have escaped the Church before it smothered him. Renzo's a free spirit. Gallivanted around Europe before getting stuck in Brussels six years ago."

"Stuck, or simply content to settle down?"

"You can ask him if you like, but Renzo's always going on about returning to his beloved Roma."

Nigel didn't tell Jenny everything. Renzo was a player. Exotic charms and a modest income from an inherited annuity were potent tools to seduce men into his bed. He didn't have a type, as far as appearance went anyway. Pretty boys and scruffy-faced hooligans were equal prey. Desperation, loneliness, and hunger were the shared traits of his conquests. "Trouble with Roma," Renzo once said to Nigel, "expensive, and loaded with Italians. How's a guy supposed to use a sexy accent to his advantage?"

Nigel motioned across the cafe. Michael sipped coffee while banging away at a laptop. "And my learned chum over there. Earned the right to live and work in the EU through his mother, an emigree from Paris to Montreal. He's an IT expert, Internet security. Books and travel are his escape. Works now and then, until he saves enough for his next adventure. Been to Sri Lanka, Thailand, and Botswana just since I've known him. Finds Brussels boring. Tired of it, as a matter of fact. But he always comes back."

"His dream?"

"Living in Paris. But distaste for full-time employment renders that more of a fantasy than an achievable goal—even if he doesn't see that himself."

"And you?"

"Me?"

"Are you waiting for the Lisbon plane?"

Nigel took a deep breath. His brown eyes widened. "Already have my ticket."

Jenny's cup paused midway between the table and her lips. "Really?"

Nigel nodded. "Several irons in the fire, as a matter of fact." He described projects ranging from inventions to screenplays to smart-phone applications. "But my focus at the moment is the launch of a charter airline. If all goes well, I'll be back in sunny Spain by Christmas."

"Barcelona?"

Nigel's lips formed a sly grin. "Perhaps."

***

Nigel Escott hurried across the nearly deserted parvis. The lead-colored sky that stalled above the city that March produced an incessant drizzle.

"Bloody Belgian climate!" he cursed as his loafers, their soles riddled with holes, sloshed into a puddle.

He stood at the bar to order a coffee and croissant but his mind was elsewhere. He pulled from his jacket a letter, but didn't open it. He didn't have to; he'd read it a dozen times. With uncharacteristic warmth and sincere sentiment, his barrister brother extended an invitation to their father's ninety-fifth birthday celebration. Shaking his head, Nigel returned the letter to his pocket. No! Can't do it. "Probably dictated to a secretary anyway," he muttered aloud.

After counting out his change, he ogled the figure of the new female server who prepared his drink. Dismissing her as a lesbian, he grabbed *The Times of London* and *El Pais* before making his way to his usual table. He greeted Renzo with a simple, "Good morning." The Italian was already seated on the banquette sipping coffee and reading *la Repubblica*, the Italian daily. A bicycle helmet rested on the table.

Renzo grinned. "Should be back in Roma before Easter." He glanced over to Michael who pored over a newspaper. "I'll fill in the details after our Canadian friend joins us."

Nigel replied with a faint smile. It wasn't the first time Renzo spoke with zeal of returning to Rome. And despite Renzo's confident tone that suggested otherwise, Nigel suspected it wouldn't be the last. Some hurdle usually surfaced. More often than not, Renzo's excuse for staying in Brussels had to do with a fresh infatuation or an overdrawn bank account.

Spreading out the newspaper, Nigel sipped his coffee. Refugee stories filled the front page. The European Union pledged unified action. Britain's new prime minister declared as top priorities, a rescue of the struggling National Health Service and a solution to the overcrowded Calais refugee camp.

An hour later, Nigel glanced up to see Michael close his newspaper. After shoving what appeared to be travel brochures into his satchel, the Canadian gathered up his bag and jacket. Watching him zigzag among the tables, Nigel wondered what might have happened to the elderly couple. Not like them. One or the other might miss the morning ritual, but never both.

After depositing his belongings, Michael dropped onto the padded bench. Nigel exchanged a look with him before both men glanced to Renzo. Each shrugged, a communal sign of bewilderment with the elderly couple's absence.

Dismissing the thought, Nigel squared his shoulders. "Well, I finished my screenplay about refugees. Sending it off to a Hollywood agent. All goes well, I'll be in Barcelona by Christmas."

Michael studied him. "Hmm, congratulations. Here I thought I had the day's best morsel."

Sitting up, Renzo leaned toward Michael. "Oh, what's that?"

"A new job."

"Paris?" Nigel asked, studying the man with skepticism and envy.

Michael swallowed hard; a blush rose in his cheeks. "N…no, Antwerp. I'll commute two days a week. Rest of the time, I'll be right here at the MDP."

Nigel and Renzo exchanged winks just as an elderly woman caused a scene at the door. She looked vaguely familiar to Nigel, perhaps a neighbor. But he wasn't certain. She'd tripped on the threshold, stopping a nasty tumble to the floor by catching the edge of a table. Startled patrons stood as their spilled beverages streamed to the floor.

Nigel returned to his mates carrying his second coffee of the morning. With shoulders slumped, his tone was sullen. "Disturbing news, I'm afraid. Quite disturbing at that." Responding to their puzzled looks, he gestured to the bar where the old woman who'd stumbled into the cafe sat on a stool. With glassy eyes, she sipped coffee using both of her shaky hands to steady the cup.

"The old couple…you know…the ones who usually sit there," Nigel added, gesturing toward Michael. "Dead." Michael and Renzo gasped. "Double suicide. Maybe just a tragic coincidence. No one knows for sure."

As his friends stared at him in silence, Nigel continued, "Been coming here for years, the old woman said. Even before it was the Maison du Peuple. Not even husband and wife. Brother and sister…imagine that. Orphaned during the war. Lived together on the parvis ever since."

Michael sighed. "What were their names?"

"Huh?"

"Their names," Renzo interjected. "What were they?"

Nigel felt his cheeks warm. "Didn't think to ask." His gaze wandered out the window, beyond his sullen reflection, and across the rain-soaked parvis to his apartment block. "I'll check the mailbox and let you know."

Responding to his mates' blank stares, he added, "They lived in my building...sixty-some-odd years. Imagine that."

A feeling of despair swept over him. How was it that for three and a half years, he never knew that the two souls who sat beside him nearly every morning lived a solitary existence one floor above him? With a wistful sigh, Nigel pushed the thought from his head and lowered himself onto the bench. His hand gently patted the pocket containing the birthday invitation as he and his mates stared vacantly ahead in silence.

One by one, they returned to their coffees and newspapers.

Nigel turned the page of *The Times of London*. A by-line caught his eye, a familiar name. "Jenny Stein. Well I'll be," he muttered aloud, recalling the pretty young blonde. I'll bed her next time for sure. His smirk vanished after reading the story's headline, "Waiting for the Lisbon Plane."

TD Arkenberg writes novels, short stories, and memoir. Organizations honoring his work include: Independent Publishers; Pirate's Alley; Next Generation Indie Books; ScreenCraft; National Indie Excellence; Eric Hoffer; and Colorado Independent Publishers. He studied at The University of Chicago, Northwestern University, and London Business School. In 2016, TD, his husband, and their Belgian cat, repatriated to Chicago.

Dimitris Politis
ALL THE MOTHERS OF THE WORLD

Beep! Beep! Beep! Beep...

Alicia's eyelids opened wide to the sound: repetitive, relentless, life draining.

How many days? How many nights? She'd lost count. Her eyes fastened on the ceiling. She struggled to move her gaze. She could barely manage a flicker. First to the right, then to the left. Everything was a blur. She tried to turn her head, to stretch her legs, but even with a strong will she was unable to control any part of her body. She could feel nothing but a familiar stiffness in her neck, condemned to remain in the same position for days on end, her head raised above the rest of her body with the help of several thick pillows.

She squeezed her eyes closed, trying to remember, trying to recall what had happened. What exactly had preceded her stay in this whitewashed hospital room? Faded images, mixed and incoherent, raced through her mind. She saw herself sitting at a desk, racked with stress, her anxious stare fixed to a computer screen. Insipid, fluorescent lights glimmered from a low ceiling. Rows of desks were separated by low partitions, a miserable plant peeking over here and there, photographs of loved ones squeezed into the corner of some desks. Waste bins overflowed with crumpled papers. Unwashed mugs. Desks stacked high with papers. And people. People all around, frantic, shouting, gesturing. Their rushed movements verged on panic. She tried to calm her mind.

The suffocating pressure of an impossible work deadline was crushing her. She remembered her distress as she worked to finish a piece for the special Sunday Edition. Her temples hurt, burning with each feverish keyboard tap. And then, disaster. All around her, angry voices and faces as she kept trying to focus on her article: "We lost the appeal to the Supreme Court." "The newspaper is closing!" "We'll be out of work! We're losing our jobs!"

She remembered trying to block her ears to the voices, turning a blind eye, hoping to shield herself from the commotion around her, resisting the dismay, the devastation, the shouts, the curses.

Now, lying helpless in her hospital bed, she heard again the sound of her fingers tapping mercilessly on the keyboard, the atmosphere around her becoming ever more hectic, increasingly violent. Her fingertips hurt as they attacked each key manically. A relentless torture she almost masochistically persisted inflicting upon herself, as if punishment for her life choices, for having decided to become a journalist, to work in a newspaper, to join this particular newspaper. Her head felt like it was exploding.

No job? My bank overdraft… my credit cards… our mortgage, our family, our future!

And then, a burning sensation filled her head. A savage, acute pain. A piercing pressure that cut short her breath. It was followed by a new kind of darkness. Then silence. For how long, she did not know, it was impossible to grasp the sense of time: seconds, minutes, days, weeks all bled into one.

This is where her memory ends. Each and every time, she is unable to untie the knots, no matter how hard she tries, no matter how many times she hopes to sew those last few minutes together. Her surroundings appear drained of all daylight. She closes her eyes.

'Does the time of day matter, really?'

Beep! Beep! Beep! Beep…

Her eyes opened again, bulging from their sockets. A renewed effort to circle the room, a desperate curiosity to explore more of the space around her. Nothing. A waste of time. She had to give-up and let her eyelids close. New images, sharper, familiar images: her husband Andrew, his eyes tearful as he's holding her hand and caressing her forehead. His face is full of tenderness and devotion as he bends towards her, whispering words that her damaged brain jumbled and jarred. His trembling voice repeats over and over again how much he loves her. In his arms is their little boy, Jason. Jason's precious green eyes, full of questions, staring at her, his lips calling out, longing for a reaction.

"Mummy... Mummy ... wake up! Mummy!... Talk to us!... Say something Mummy!"

His tiny fingers try to touch her, clumsily making contact with her face. The terrible agony of her inability to reply, to touch them back, to put their minds at ease. The agony of not being able to ask their forgiveness for the pain she was causing them. How she wanted to sit upright, to jump out of that damn bed and shout, "I'm alright! I'm going to be alright!" It didn't seem to matter what she wanted any more, her body was refusing to obey.

Beep! Beep! Beep! Beep...

The strain of holding her eyes open became too much. With great effort, she managed to swallow. Her saliva tasted bitter, poisonous, but with this swallowing came a change. A ray of hope, perhaps, she could swallow by herself; she could fill her lungs with oxygen without mechanical help. These realizations helped her to push on, motivated her to escape the white prison, from the blinding spotlight of her bedrest lamp. She managed to flee, to transport her mind to another time, another dimension. New images from years ago flooded back, more colourful and vivid this time. She saw herself as a twenty-something university student, squeezed into an uncomfortable economy plane seat, onboard an overcrowded flight from New Delhi to London.

She was exhausted boarding that Air India flight, requiring assistance from her country's consulate after falling sick with a stomach virus. All her possessions had been stolen while on the train ride to her yoga school in Rishikesh. She relived the sensation of enormous fatigue, the nausea, the sweat, the dehydration and the stomach cramps. The unbearable humidity that made breathing a challenge. The feeling of helplessness. And those two nights she'd spent penniless, on a filthy bench at the railway station, surrounded by strange, curious, ragged people. Wounded animals wandered around her in their desperate search for food.

She recalled the moment she was offered the plastic tray of airline food by the hostess, a forced smile. She remembered the discreet look of the dark-skinned stranger seated beside her. His thick, shiny hair, his compassionate eyes witnessing the scene, his lack of courage to intervene.

She remembered herself sometime later, curled-up in the narrow seat, trying to cover her cold limbs with a tiny blanket. At times, she glanced through the plane windows at the great celestial mass as it lost its brightness turning from a faded blue to a black cloak embroidered with shiny silver sparkles. She remembered waking-up now and again, as the muted fuselage made its smooth flight through the night. During one of these waking moments she watched the lady sitting next to her sacrifice her own blanket to keep her warm. The lady caressed her forehead from time to time, and gave her a gentle, encouraging smile. The kind old man on her other side, whispered in his distinctive accent, "Everything will be fine. Your mother has sent all the mothers of the world to look after you tonight!"

A hundred more haemorrhages would not be enough to wipe out his soothing words. She remembers feeling a new lightness; relief, almost free from the symptoms of her terrible suffering. She was able to find for the first time in days a deep and restful sleep until awakened by the jolt of the plane as its wheels touched down onto the wet tarmac of a Heathrow runway. She recalled the first words of her tearful mother as they fell into each other's arms in the Arrivals Hall, "You were a thousand miles away but my mind was with you each and every second."

Her eyes opened.

Beep! Beep! Beep! Beep…

The same repetitive beep. The same fog. The same whitewashed twilight. None of it mattered anymore. In that moment she had a revelation. 'I will be able to look after Jason in the same way.' Like her mother, she would use all the mothers of the world to protect her child, to keep him safe, to help him become the adult she hoped he'd one day be. When he needed her, through the power of her heart, the power of her inexhaustible love, she would be there for him.

'Nothing can ever separate me from my little Jason! Ever...' her dry lips attempted to smile. At that moment, her body shook violently. She felt the same burning sensation in her head, the same unbearable siege of her skull, the one she'd felt for the first time at her desk. But she did not panic this time. The harsh, unyielding light of the sterile room melted into the whites of her eyes.

Everything became silent except the hospital monitor next to her bed: *Beep! Beep! Beep! Beeeeeeeeeeeeeeeee…*

Dimitris Politis is from Athens, Greece. He studied Economics in Greece, and Classics & Literature in Ireland. He has published short stories, three of which have won literary competitions. He has two novels published: *The stolen life of a cheerful man* (2014) and *The Next Stop* (2019).

Teodora Lalova
ONE SPRING

Spring has come accordant to the calendar,
But, as I have tried to explain for a while now,
real spring is on a different path. This one here, right now,
smells like spring and sounds like spring, and the trees and the evenings
have blossomed into heavy promises. And yet,
whenever I give spring my hand – for I want to touch it and thus make it mine – it eludes me.

The reasons have something to do with my body
which still breathes a time zone away.
Only a baby time zone, I'll admit, merely an hour difference;
nothing too insistent. And there are certain keys
that tune my hands and my lips, no, my eyes
to my present coordinates.

Like the act of learning French,
a friend's house after sunset, the lights dim and the fire crackling
or spending an afternoon at the museum,
in front of a picture of the sea, the waves crashing in 1878.
Or the view out my window very early in the morning,

just before I leave for the station.

But the body is stubborn. It takes pleasure in hearing the wind caressing scented lilacs in the Tsar's garden some 2000 km away.
That is the *real* voice of spring.
I don't know why, then, once I do step under the lilacs
that I feel as if spring has eluded me once again.

Teodora Lalova, Bulgarian, currently lives in Brussels where she is doing a PhD in Law, in collaboration with KU Leuven and EORTC. She obtained her LL.M. from KU Leuven and holds a Master of Laws diploma from Sofia University (Bulgaria). Teodora writes poetry in English and Bulgarian, and is a laureate of several national poetry competitions.

Larisa Doctorow
THE IMMORTAL REGIMENT

My family lived in St. Petersburg for the whole of the 20th century and, like everyone I knew, they were forever marked by the dramatic events of the time: I refer to the Revolution of 1917, the widespread starvation that followed, and the siege of 1941-1943.

In Russia, the Second World War was known locally as The Great Patriotic War, and as far back as I can remember, the 9th May - the day that war ended - was always specially marked. On the morning of 9th May, every city in the country held a military parade, followed by public gatherings called by labor unions and other agents of the Party.

After several hours spent at these officially organized events, relatives and friends would come to our apartment for a sit-down dinner. My parents liked having guests and spared no effort to please them, always setting the most splendid table. The main entertainment was of course the conversation, but there were also songs from members of my aunt's family. And there were poetry readings from a revered guest, Vladimir Zotov, who was a relative of my father's. These festive days always concluded with fireworks.

With the fall of Communism, public gatherings like ours disappeared and so did many large family dinners. Certainly, there were other occasions to get together, like Easter, Christmas and New Year's Eve. But in my family, the 9th of

May had always been special, an intermix of joy and sadness as we remembered the battles fought and celebrated the victories and the lives of our dear ones lost. It was a tradition we did not wish to part with. It was not just the symbolism of the day that attracted me, but the importance of the connection to a time in my family's, and indeed, the entire country's history.

Four years ago, an unexpected movement of civil society, called the 'March of the Immortal Regiment', was initiated in Siberia and went on to inspire millions of people across the country. The march began as a way to unite families in commemorating their loved ones. All over the country people took to the streets, carrying portraits of their relatives who participated in the Second World War. It was an initiative I wholeheartedly adopted and to this day travel from my home in Brussels to participate along side remaining family members and friends.

My father and his three brothers fought in that war. Two of them never returned. My grandmother, Efrosinia, lost her husband, my grandfather, whom I never met. Her son, my uncle Mikhail, went to war as a young conscript. Mikhail was drafted when he was barely nineteen. At the start of the war, he was severely wounded and lost a leg. I remember his anguish with prostheses. I carry his picture, which shows a young, curly-haired, smiling man, his face unmarked by the atrocities of the war.

But it wasn't just the men who served. During the war my grandmother spent many years working at St Petersburg's

Erismann Hospital, firstly as a technician, then as a doctor-radiologist. When I was a child, Efrosinia was my link to my family's past, often recounting heroic stories of the ones we lost. But, I regret, in my childhood I barely listened to her stories.

In 1940, my father graduated from the Frunze Naval Academy and was assigned to Vladivostok, in the Far East. He could have chosen any seaside city in the country, but my adventurous parents decided they wanted to see the Pacific Ocean. Initially, my father went alone, expecting his wife to join shortly. The war started all of a sudden in June 1941 and my mother managed to get a seat on one of the last trains leaving Leningrad and traveling south to Moscow.

In his first posting, my father worked as the head of a meteorological station located on the hills near Vladivostok. From the outbreak of the war, he was navigating ships that transported cargo across the ocean from San Francisco to Vladivostok. Of course, they were in constant danger of running into Japanese sea mines.

At the start of August 1941, Efrosinia's hospital unit was sent to the Leningrad front, and she spent the war years close to the battle fields. In September 1941, the German troops closed their armed ring around the city. After the Germans surrendered, there was no rest. Efrosinia's hospital was loaded onto a train and dispatched to the Far East, where the war with Japan raged on. Japan's capitulation caught them in Siberia. I remember my father and my grandmother often arguing over who between them was the greater hero: my father who served on a ship near Murmansk in the Barents Sea, or Efrosinia who witnessed the ravages of land battles and bandaged wounds on the front lines.

The most difficult months for residents of Leningrad were from December 1941 up to March 1942, a period marked by hundreds of thousands of deaths. Food rationing began in the autumn; by December the bread ration was reduced to 125 grams per person per day. In December 1941, my great-grandmother died. Valentina, my aunt, who at the start of the war was just 10 years old, later told me about it: "I asked grandmother why she refused her piece of bread and each time she replied, 'I am not hungry. You eat it'. Of course, I gulped it down. After a few days, she was dead. Only later did I realize what she was doing."

In February 1942, Valentina had been evacuated on the *Road of Life*, the trail crossing the frozen Lake Ladoga. She was one of 1,300,000 inhabitants who escaped death by starvation. She came back to the city in 1945. All her life she recalled blockade soup made from joiner's glue. It seemed to her so delicious, that her dream was to one day, when she grew-up, have this soup every day. I think that for the next March of the Immortal Regiment I will carry a picture of her. She was not at war, but spent part of her childhood in the besieged Leningrad and was later awarded a medal.

In 1944, my father was transferred to the Northern Fleet, where he participated in the joint Russian-British convoys transporting goods to Russia under the Lend Lease program. Vladimir Zotov was an architect and never held a weapon in his hands. When the war broke-out, he was drafted into the People's Militia to protect Pulkovo Heights on the outskirts of St Petersburg. He was badly injured, though I don't know how, and all his life suffered from wounds on his legs. His photograph is one of the three I carry when I march. But preparing photographs for the march is not easy.

In the hamlet of Orlino, some 80 km south of Petersburg where our summerhouse is, I asked neighbors for advice on where I could prepare photos for the march. They gave me the address of a photo-shop in the neighboring town of Siversk. The next morning, I went there early. I was grateful to find myself ahead of a crowd of townsfolk who had gathered at the steps of the shop. We were all there for the same purpose, bringing along pictures of relatives who had died in the war.

The next day I travelled to St. Petersburg by train. In each railcar, there were dozens of people with their dear heroes looking out over the tops of hand-held white poles. In the metro within the city, the crowds grew and grew. It seemed that the whole city was moving in the same direction.

We arrived at the Alexander Nevsky Square, the marshalling point of the march. People were joining the procession slowly moving towards the city center. The portraits of our Immortal Regiment were held high. The first two kilometers of Nevsky Prospect - the main artery of the city - starting from Alexander Nevsky Square, were lined with high fashion boutiques, and because the street is not as wide as the mid-point - Uprising Square - it was a pretty dense crowd.

As we moved along, we thinned out a bit. Some people were carrying flags, some sheets of paper with the names of those who had died written out in careful penmanship.

I found out later that 300, 000 people took part in the St. Petersburg march. Despite the large numbers, I didn't feel any discomfort. Everything was orderly, and we moved along at a calm gait, with frequent stops. The mood was always festive if not solemn. From time to time a wave of shouts of "Hurrah!" passed down our column and back again. At times people broke into popular Russian songs, mostly "Katyusha." I proudly carried the portraits of my father and my grandmother. My husband, who walked alongside me, carried a portrait of my uncle. The pictures were respectfully decorated. Large and laminated, the St. George's ribbon - a symbol of Russian military valor - in each upper right corner.

There were families consisting of two and three generations. Several small children were pushed in strollers or carried in their parents' arms. In the windows of some houses were photos of men in military uniforms who, while not dead, were too sick or old to go down into the streets themselves. By exhibiting pictures in the windows, the families were showing their support and sympathy as if they were themselves marching in the street.

As we walked, I shared stories about the war, particularly the Siege. Doing so revived the names of those long gone and brought childhood stories back to my memory. It felt good to remember things I thought had slipped away. My beloved father lived and died in the city. When he suffered a stroke and was carried to the hospital by ambulance, he stretched his face to the window hoping for one last glance of the city he loved. He muttered, "My last walk through Petersburg."

I thought of him as I carried his photograph, 'Daddy, that was not your last walk. With me, you'll walk every May, and after me, with your granddaughter'. I could think of no greater tribute to my favourite among the Immortal Regiment.

Larisa Doctorow née Zalesova is a journalist and music critic. For more than 20 years she has published in both English and Russian print media and online resources. Her second novel *The Mosaic of My Life* has just been published in Russia. Doctorow lives in Brussels and St. Petersburg.

Sean Gibson
HOW LONG IS LONG ENOUGH

If I could live once more my life, I would
But dream of finding one such one again.
The one that quickened once a distant thud
Of pressure in a long-neglected vein.

I dream of finding one such one again,
Have faith that you can stitch it where it tore;
Of pressure in a long-neglected vein.
Your searing needle always leaves me sore.

Have faith that you can stitch it where it tore,
Though every inch of thread is sure to hurt;
That searing needle will always leave me sore
Of hands that hammer doors until they're heard.

Though every mile of thread is sure to hurt
The one who quickened once a distant thud
Of hands that hammer doors until they're heard,
If I could live once more my life.

SHE TOLD ME SO

Impressions on the wood are getting harder to trace,
Her weight upon the boards has long since stepped away,
I always said I never learnt to savour the chase;
But what peace in rest, in lying where she lay?

I'll have to brace myself and make for the door,
To follow her route, cross these streets alone,
Don the hat and scarf she wished I'd worn,
Then swap our cooling boards for the frostbitten stone.

Outside; and when I fail to find her on land
I'll try the sea, where she was a favoured guest;
And when we cross back over, I swear we'll hold hands,
I promise – cross my heart, or my vacant chest.

Beyond this threshold I cannot know
How far I have to go; but I will find her – she told me so.

CHILDREN

Naming names and

framing faces

Makes them much more real

and less so;

Pencilled in familiar places,

Naming names and

framing faces

Of their own;

the worry traces

Lines that memory can't yet know,

though

Naming names and

framing faces

Makes them much more real

and less so.

Sean Gibson is a writer from Manchester, United Kingdom. Although he has worked as a journalist, creative writing was his first love. In school Sean had poetry published in Manchester Metropolitan University's *All Write!* anthology each year from 2005-2009. Most recently, Earlyworks Press published three of his pieces in their anthology *Origami Poems and Towering Stories.*

Manuel Delgado
BIRTHDAY IN HER EYES

eyelashes framed the venue
shiny eyelids for the party
eyebrows were the crowds

blinking a round of applause
among tearing glimpses
night arrived; illuminating pupils

and the horizon of time
was the colour of your iris
the rest was White

and I said, again,
Blanca
happy birthday

WAR AT SWEET NIGHTFALL

Bruges. Scattered like soldiers, no guns,
just brushes and combs, lipsticks and razors, that's all,
souls spread like mines; for us, moons are suns
bright uniforms ready, war comes at sweet nightfall

smelling sounds, tasting words, a trap, no doubt
drink your judgment, become your avatar
fight great battles, not even hearts go out;
heels high as hills, guerrilla land, the bar

smiles in a series of beats - passion
clashing glasses, patience is cold to hold
the theme: kiss a smile, an eye, a mood - fashion
dress to undress, dig for secret gold

last minutes, come on! The show must go-go on
Hidalgo! Drink all at once, it´s our song

Manuel Delgado studied Law & Political Science at ICADE in 2015, has an MA in International Relations from the Spanish Diplomatic School and an MA in European Political Studies from the College of Europe. A Brussels-based Spanish professional, Manuel has become an outsider artist focused on the "Art Writing" discipline through poetry.

Alexandros Yannis
THE WAR AND THE WALL

"War," Kostis said. "Waarrr," he repeated emphatically.

He was lying on the sofa in the living room, surfing the Internet on his tablet. He glanced at Lisa as she entered the flat to pick up a few personal things she'd left behind and to hand over her keys. She looked at him, no hint of surprise at what he was saying or the intensity of his words. Kostis was like that.

They had lived together, though only for a few months, and every time she entered the flat, instead of greeting her with a "hello," Kostis would launch into some political or philosophical monologue. This was often like being greeted by a storm that would last deep into the night.

Now in his late 40s, Kostis had lost pace but none of his passion. Tonight, Lisa didn't move to kiss him the way she always did upon entering the flat. Though she was more than ten years younger, she knew how to handle separation.

"I just finished an article about the subliminal power of first memories. And just as you were coming in, I remembered my oldest memory. The very first memory I can put a date and place on," Kostis said, never stopping to pause.

Lisa took off her coat and placed the keys on the small table near the entrance. She walked into the bedroom and went to gather-up the clothes she'd forgotten in a rarely used chest of drawers. Kostis knew the purpose of her visit and for this reason his stomach was in knots. But he too had experience in breaking-up and he knew how to behave.

"The invasion of Cyprus by Turkish troops was my very first memory. July 1974. I was just five years old," Kostis said in a loud voice to make sure she could hear him from the bedroom.

Lisa returned to the living room and placed a bag of clothes on the floor. She sat on the far edge of the sofa, smiling at him in a knowing way. She wasn't about to spoil his desire to talk, not under the circumstances. She would make an effort because it was the last time. She was German, from East Berlin, born much later than the story Kostis was in the process of relaying. She nodded, intrigued by this history lesson, silently urging him to continue.

"It was a hot summer day on the balcony of my family's flat in Athens. Everybody was distressed. My mother was pacing between the kitchen and balcony, carrying things that nobody had asked for or needed. My father was painting the balcony tiles each one over and over again at a frenetic pace. There were some quiet moments, I recall, when everyone turned their ears to the radio which was alive with military songs interspersed with news from the war."

Lisa leaned toward Kostis and rested her chin in her hand. His engaging character was one of the reasons she fell in love with him; love at first sight you might say. She loved his passion for discussion, his openness; he was a diplomat after all, and diplomats talk for a living. "Diplomacy can rarely resolve conflicts, but by keeping dialogue alive, it can often prevent them from getting worse," Kostis liked to say. All these qualities initially pleased her.

"I remember that my uncle had been called up by the Greek army and the presence of my aunt heightened the distress on the balcony. I don't remember my elder brothers; they were probably around, but memory, as you know, can be selective and capricious. I guess, not that different from dreams. I do remember, however, that I was lying in a corner of the balcony playing with football figures. But even as a small boy, I could feel the tension. I was uncharacteristically quiet," said Kostis, followed by a self-depreciating chuckle.

Lisa smiled and fidgeted. She wanted to collect her bag of forgotten clothes and leave. But before she could initiate her departure, Kostis continued with his recollection, partly because he wanted to talk, but also because he didn't want her to leave. Once again, Lisa felt trapped; a rabbit frozen in Kostis' headlights.

"Many people claim to know with some certainty their earliest memory. I guess the stronger the emotions, the deeper the impressions. I probably had an uneventful childhood until this first memory, perhaps just a happy one. But my little protective cocoon burst that day. The first memory, in a way, is the day I was really born." Kostis became pensive and his gaze drifted away from Lisa.

Lisa was aware that she had not yet uttered a single word, but in her silence, she felt very close to Kostis. Relationships are magical things. That is perhaps why people talk about chemistry when they want to describe something that happens between two people. Lisa believed she was still in love with him, but something inside her, something she couldn't put a finger on, told her that their differences could never be reconciled and that it was time for her to move on.

She vacillated between getting up to leave and staying a little bit longer, not because she had any second thoughts, but because under the circumstances and while both knew how to behave, just under the surface, she sensed there was still tension.

Kostis also was still in love with her and he hadn't figured out what exactly had gone wrong between them; what was behind the break-up. He took at face value her view that they were simply not made to be together. Nonetheless, he wanted her to stay a bit longer. He put the laptop aside and started slowly walking around the room, his eyes gazing into the corners. Walking often gave him additional energy to talk, like a bicycle dynamo, and tonight he felt he needed more energy.

"This very first memory is perhaps why I hate war so much. And why I am such a hopeless peacenik. Why I believe in compromise and not bravado. Why I believe in openness and the abolition of borders and barriers. Perhaps, this is the reason I believe in the European Union. The world's ultimate peace project."

Lisa realised that this discussion, this monologue to be more accurate, wasn't going to end anytime soon. She manoeuvred herself into a more comfortable position on the sofa and fixed her eyes on Kostis. Deep inside she knew that these passionate discussions were somehow part of the problem in their relationship and why she wanted to end it. And yet, as much as they repelled her, at the same time they drew her in, for reasons she couldn't explain. She believed that something was either right or wrong, but her relationship with Kostis fell into some unfamiliar grey area that was neither.

Lisa felt under siege by the way Kostis circled the sofa. Like Kostis, Lisa also believed in the idea of Europe, but differently and up to a point. She also believed in countries and borders as a way of preserving traditions and keeping order. And war wasn't her concern; war was something that happened elsewhere, something she watched on television or read about in the news.

Kostis' voice burst into her thoughts as if he knew what she was thinking.

"The less one knows about war, the less one fears it. Perhaps it would be helpful if everybody's first memory was about war. Maybe then there would be fewer wars in the world?"

Lisa smiled in reply, not because she fully understood or agreed with his point, but because she found that smiling always helped. It also disguised the fact that her mind was drifting elsewhere. Kostis' story about his first memory and his view about its subliminal influence prompted her to think back to her own first memory.

"The link you are trying to make between your first memory and the European Union is a fascinating one. For once, it's a story from your heart and not from your brain." With these words Lisa suddenly switched from being a passive listener to an active participant and she knew exactly what she wanted to say next.

"How about a drink and a bite to eat? I'm starving. And psychoanalysis on an empty stomach doesn't suit me."

"That is a brilliant idea," Kostis replied, eager to continue the conversation, not only because discussion was his oxygen, but also because he didn't want this last night together to end anytime soon.

A couple of minutes later, they were on their way out, Lisa carrying the bag of clothing she'd come to the flat to collect. She hoped, over the course of their evening, to explore her own first memory. It might go some way to explaining why she was leaving him.

It was eerily quiet outside. They opted for a bar they'd frequented many times together just a five-minute walk from the flat. The place was deserted so they had their pick of the tables. They chose one in the corner by a window that didn't allow people to sit facing each other but only side-by-side. They both loved this table as they found it more intimate. Proximity enhances desire. They ordered two Negroni and some tapas.

As they waited for drinks Lisa made a joke, wondering what first memories could be responsible for them both preferring to sit next to each other rather than opposite, as most couples do. Kostis replied, in a serious tone, that first memories didn't dictate the future but only influenced it. The dynamic of the conversation had changed.

"Wall," said Lisa. "Waaall," she repeated emphatically, imitating the tone of the first words of Kostis back in the flat. "The fall of the Berlin Wall is my first memory. I was four years old and living with my parents in East Berlin. And it fell on the wrong side. Because the only thing I remember from that night was my mother screaming into the phone. She'd learned that my father, a high government official at the time, had just committed suicide. I was a few meters away from her and I remember her screaming, cursing everything and everybody around her until she fell to the floor and was silent." Lisa spoke in a very matter-of-fact tone, the entire time looking over her shoulder into Kostis' eyes.

"I think I remember that she also cursed the fall of the Berlin Wall, but probably, this is a memory that over time I have mixed-up so now I no longer know what's true and what my mind has made-up. Memories are not only selective and capricious as you've said, but also deceitful." She smiled and took a sip of her drink.

Lisa's eloquence, she was a lawyer after all, were part of the reasons Kostis had fallen in love with her. And while he was resigned to the truth of them splitting up, he remained eager to discover how a couple with so much in common could have fallen apart so quickly. This discussion about first memories had cracked some light into a dark corner of her soul. A place he'd never been before. He wanted to hear more. He ordered a second round of drinks and turned his gaze to her, all the while hoping that the power of alcohol to loosen the tongue would work in his favour now.

"I never found out the real reason for my father's suicide. My mother, who had a nervous breakdown a short while later, never really recovered. She died a few years after that, always insisting that my father was a true believer who simply couldn't stand the fall of Communism. But growing-up I also heard stories and insinuations that my father was implicated in some nasty things." Tears formed in her eyes.

"I am sorry," is all that Kostis could manage to say as he stretched an arm around her shoulder.

"The fall of the Berlin Wall was for me a traumatic experience, whether my father was a good or a bad person makes no difference. This memory has marked me; it turned my life upside down. You are the one who loves analysing things, what does this first memory say about me, eh?" Lisa asked while recovering her composure somewhat in the realization that it may be that her fear of openness and her yearn for barriers was the result of this early trauma.

Kostis accepted the challenge but he needed time to think before expressing an opinion. These were delicate moments, and this made him nervous. To gain some time, he stood to go to the restroom, reassuring her that upon his return he would share his thoughts.

He entered the bathroom and locked the door. Looking in the mirror he saw the aged man he had become. 'It would be nice if mirrors could reflect our memories,' he thought, 'We would always look our most youthful; face to face with our past. Then maybe we would also better understand what we have become? But would knowing our past change the present?' He splashed water on his face and dried it with a paper towel.

Kostis stepped from the restroom with a clear head only to find an empty table; Lisa and her bag were gone. For the first time, and probably for the last time, he felt he truly understood her.

"The wall fell on the wrong side," he uttered to himself. "Would it have helped if I had known this earlier? Possibly." Kostis sat and stared out the window, a bittersweet smile forming on his lips.

Alexandros Yannis was born in Athens in 1969 and has lived and worked in Geneva, Nairobi, Somalia, New York, Kosovo and Boston. He is a European diplomat and he currently lives in Brussels. He has published widely on international relations and is also the author of the novel and political thriller *Chimera*.

Xavier Queipo
KOTARO

One hand caressing the other.
An old armchair delimits time
from emptiness.
Chopsticks over a bowl of rice.
Loneliness.
A distant agoraphobic look.

One leaf from a male ginkgo
floats in a vast pool where Buddha rests.
Virtual territory for banned love.
Horsehair brush designing ideograms.
Love.
Word to grasp when fear attacks.

Purple leaves falling from a dying tree
moments before it collapses.
Drops slipping on the mirror of time.
Subjective coordinates.
Unity.
Absolute new dimension.

Self-mutilation, cutting the flesh.
Martyrdom or fidelity?
Shared madness with a bloody back shining.
Madness.
Little heart of jade.

Ceremony of time, of love
and solitude.
Blood dropping into
the pond of sacred turtles and nenuphars.
Loyalty.
Wakashu, My Dear Wakashu.

ME NOT DARING TO TALK TO YOU

SHY   Cautious like the swimming of a black halibut in the burning desert of Arizona.
Laconic inside the protection of a hermit crab's shell.

SILENT   Soft as a kite on its declining flight.
Yellow as the flowers that blossom in April.
Attached to somebody's fin, like an obstinate parasitic remora.

MUTE   Swimming like a whale shark in the bottom of the calcareous forest.
Speechless.
Wisdom equals 'no action'. Dancing with pink jellyfish in the depths of oceanic reefs.

TIMID   Speechless. Bashful.
The water reveals the sea urchins secretly encrusted in walls of stone.

TERSE   Apprehensive. Yellow.
Foam transports bleeding seaweed, dyeing water over the warmth of a glorious night.

DISTANT   Silent. Mute.
           Blackish crabs of velvet carapaces walking
                               infuriated towards the cliffs.
           Me not daring to talk to you.

Xavier Queipo (Galice, 1957). Regularly writes in Galician. Publications: *Ártico*, short stories, 1990, *O Paso do Noroeste*, novel, 1996; *O ladrón de esperma*, short stories, 2001; *Extramunde*, novel, 2011 and *Os kowa*, novel, 2016. *Kite* (Small Stations, 2018) is his first novel translated to English. Awarded with the Spanish Critics Award (1991), and the Spanish National Prize of Translation (2014).

Katja Knežević
THE DINNER

"Let's have some wine before we head off," Yasmin said, uncorking the bottle. Her face and arms twisted with the effort. I could see that she felt comfortable in my kitchen and I liked that. I leaned out the windowsill blowing puffs of smoke into the spring sunset.

"Sure, but shouldn't we leave soon?" I stubbed my cigarette into the potted plant on the sill, turning away from the smoke. Yasmin spun between the kitchen bar and the cabinets, holding a wine glass in each hand, using two fingers to pinch the rims. She set them on the bar and bent her index finger at me in invitation.

My flat at the time was an oversized shoebox, a tiny cube of freedom. The bar pretended to be a wall between the kitchen and the rest of the place. The study, the living room, and the bedroom were all mashed into twenty square metres of space.

I watched her pour the wine. She was wearing jeans and a black lace bra. I could see her ribcage, and her breastbone jumped up and down as she laughed. She didn't seem to mind, not wearing a blouse in front of me. My lips twisted, suppressing a content smile – I knew myself; feeling hopeful meant looking hopeful.

"I just texted Celine to tell her we'll be late," she winked. I smiled.

***

I first met Yasmin almost a year ago. She had just returned to Brussels and called one of her friends for drinks. Her casual invitation quickly escalated: a friend brought a colleague, and the colleague brought a boyfriend, and the boyfriend brought a random person he'd met the night before, etc. I was one of the tag-alongs in what ended up being a very large group.

We commandeered several tables on a terrace of a bar in the centre of town, pulled them together into an island, and quickly began to make the rounds of "what-do-you-do", "where-are-you-from", "how long are you in town?" Occasionally, I would sit back in my chair and sip on my cocktail, watching the others in action. I liked people watching. I still do.

Yasmin came to the party late. She was half-announced by her friend, only to me it turns out. He waved and smiled at her then quickly mumbled in my ear "She can be intense. I mean, I adore her, but just so you know."

She approached half-skipping, half-walking, chirping apologies and hellos, blowing kisses as she circled the table. I remember she was dressed in black jeans and a black short-sleeved top. Her hazel eyes were enormous and she had wild, chestnut brown hair.

She sat beside her friend and swallowed him whole. He didn't talk to me the rest of the evening, seemingly captivated by everything Yasmin said. I watched her over his shoulder, drawn by her story. At times, she looked straight at me, the only acknowledgment of my presence. And whenever she did, she would quickly, almost imperceptibly, lick her lips. Each time I felt myself blush.

Drinks turned into dinner and dinner turned into more drinks. Over time, people from the group disappeared. I felt hot, which made me drink more. I wiped my forehead with the back of my hand, all the while staying zoomed in on Yasmin. Eventually, of our original group there were two girls on the other side of the table, and they were deep in their conversation. Yasmin came and sat next to me. As she chain-smoked, her many bracelets and earrings jangled. She continued unravelling the last year of her life in words, as if offering it to me, to understand, or accept, or perhaps envy. I did all three.

She was a dancer. Or, more precisely, was going to be one. After quitting the conservatory in The Hague, just months before graduating, she fled to Amsterdam.

"Oh, Kate, I couldn't bear it any longer," she swapped my name 'Katarzyna' with 'Kate' without so much as batting an eyelid. I wasn't sure if she did it on purpose or simply didn't remember my name. I accepted it with a suppressed chuckle, as she continued, "I suffered for months. I cannot tell you how it… it destroyed me. Maybe it was all the rules. Or the idea that I would always have to contain myself to belong to a… to this… I don't know, structure. Anyway. It made me hate dancing. And, of course, myself."

Yasmin had thrown herself into the bloodstream of Amsterdam, drowning her doubts in sensations, substances, and people. Several hazy weeks later, she woke up in somebody's flat. She decided she needed a cleanse. She booked a one-way ticket to Patna, her father's birth town, where she retreated to a yoga centre.

"It was the best and the worst month of my life, I have to tell you. I was alone. I saw myself for what I really am. It was painful. And I wouldn't trade it for anything."

There she met a forty-two-year-old former CFO who had suffered burnout and wanted to start his life from scratch.

"I was totally gone for the man! It was like somebody put blinkers on my head. My entire world began and ended with him… We travelled a lot." She paused to slowly exhale smoke, "He was so caring.

"And now, we'll see! I love this city so much, it's absolutely amazing," she glanced down at her mojito and stirred the ice cubes with a bent straw. "I want to do something that involves people, you know?"

"Yeah, I understand that. I mean, I work with…"

"I am sorry, Kate, you have the most gorgeous eyes," she interrupted me, sounding as if she'd only that moment noticed. "Has anyone told you that? Sorry, you were saying, you work with someone?" She smiled the widest smile at me.

I chuckled, both confused and flattered, suddenly overcome with the need to know what else she noticed about me. Our evening ended too soon, and as much as I wanted to see her again, it would be another eight months before she made contact.

"Oh, Kate, sweety, I'm so sorry, I won't make it to the party tonight."

"Can we actually postpone the dinner?"

"I am going through something."

"Next time for sure."

"We'll catch up, I promise."

"So sorry."

"No."

* * *

April came. The air was stuffy, the city cramped, the streets were wet. I was sorting through books in my little flat when my phone rang. When I saw Yasmin's name, I flinched and let it ring a bit longer before answering.

"Hello?" I said, as if I didn't know.

"Kate?"

"Yes?" I tried to keep a neutral tone.

"What is your address?"

"I'm sorry?"

"Your address. Give it to me."

Her voice was shaky. There was a buzzing sound in the background. Was she in a car? I gave her my address and hung up. I smelled my armpits, then put on some perfume. I stood in front of the mirror, let my hair down, put it back in a bun, then let it down again.

The doorbell rang.

Yasmin had lost a lot of weight, as if she had any to lose. She looked pale, with too much blush on her cheeks. The strands of green and brown in her eyes that used to intertwine in a curious dance now hid behind a haze.

"Can I stay with you for a few days?" She asked before I had stepped aside to let her in.

She entered my territory and quickly made it hers. Or rather, I made it hers for her. Whatever I cooked, I checked with her first. I was suddenly buying red wine. Any conversation I started, I made sure it was vague enough, so that she could steer it in the direction of her choosing. We stayed up late every night, talking about films, my job, her ex-partners. I had no idea how long this would last – or what it was – so I made every day matter. I liked functioning like that. It felt natural.

One evening, as we sat on the sofa that doubled as Yasmin's bed, watching *Black Swan*, Yasmin was texting someone. Even when she put the phone down on the table, she would glance at it every few minutes.

"Sorry, what's going on now?" she asked, pointing at the TV.

"She just got the part. She's calling her mother," I said, trying not to show my irritation.

Yasmin wrapped herself in a blanket and put her head in my lap. Her hair spilled over my thighs like seagrass swept across a sandy shore. We stayed like this, watching in silence until her phone rang. She declined the call. A few minutes later it rang again. This time she turned the phone off. After a while, I heard her sniffling.

I whispered: "Yasmin, who was that?"

"My mom," she said after a pause.

I lowered my head closer to hers. "Don't you want to talk to her?"

"I do," she sobbed, "honestly."

"Shall we call her back?" I added myself to the equation.

She jumped up and started rocking back and forth. "No, no, no… I can't! I can't!"

"What do you mean? Has she done something to you?"

"God, no, not her! It was me! It's always me." She stopped rocking, but she cried so hard I thought she might stop breathing. I put my hand on her shoulder.

"Yasmin, I can't help you if you don't tell me…"

She jumped and looked at me frowning, her face red and wet. "I didn't ask you to help me."

I wanted to poke her and point out that she had been sleeping on my sofa, but she kept her unblinking stare on me. I stretched my lips into a cautious smile. "I'm sorry. Really, it's none of my business."

"Exactly."

She put her head back in my lap. I tried to focus on the film, my thoughts pulsing into Natalie Portman's bloodied twirl. When I felt Yasmin's breathing had relaxed, I put my hand on her shoulder.

* * *

"It's... Mark, right? Celine's fiancé?"

We had finished the bottle and were about to head for the restaurant.

"That's right. You'll see, Celine is absolutely amazing. I think you will like her," Yasmin said, smiling and squinting.

"Why?" I gulped down my wine.

"I don't know. I mean, it would be impossible not to. She's a motherly-type too." She answered before putting her top on.

"Oh." *Too.* We left the apartment.

My head was spinning. Yasmin put her sunglasses on and strutted down the street, her right arm on her hip, her left arm in the air. I burst out laughing.

Celine and Mark were waiting for us at a nearby Italian bistro. The street was filled with the sounds of clinking glasses, fluttering menus, and Yasmin's laughter.

"Yasmin, you need to eat! So thin!" Celine said with a sharp French accent, frowning at Yasmin from the moment we reached their table.

"Well, we are in a restaurant, mummy dearest," Yasmin chirped, then turned to me. "See? What did I tell you?" Celine rolled her eyes and smiled. She had a long nose and clear blue eyes, and a wave of dark blond hair. Mark also rolled his eyes, but not with the same benevolence as Celine.

The couple had been planning their wedding, so we spent a good half-hour talking about florists and location scouting, and indulged in a unanimous lament of the unpredictability of the Brussels weather. I became bored very quickly which made me want to drink more.

Mark said Brussels was almost 'unbearably' small when compared to New York, but he had to admit it had a certain *zhwah duh veev-ruh* he enjoyed. For some reason, that led him into giving us a 20-minute-long comparative analysis of 9/11 in the US and the terrorist attacks in Brussels. He was such an American stereotype – the kind I used to see in films when I was little – it was bordering on hilarious. Light brown hair, high forehead, square nose, thin lips. Quarterback-cheerleader's-boyfriend-business-school-type. I wondered why Yasmin would know someone this boring? Is it a matter of balance in the universe?' I laughed out loud just as Mark was making his way through the final stages of al-Qaeda's history. "I am so sorry," I stammered, and hid behind my glass. Yasmin looked at me with a mixture of relief and amusement. Celine threw apologetic looks somehow at both Mark and me, but used the opportunity to shift the conversation back to Yasmin.

"Darling, how long are you staying with Kate?"

"I don't know, we'll see. I like it there."

"I see. If you need anything, you know that…"

"I know."

There was an awkward silence. We all dipped into our glasses. Yasmin twitched as if she remembered something. "Excuse me," she said, then pushed her chair back and went to the toilet. Celine followed with her eyes and, the moment

Yasmin disappeared, she turned and whispered, "Katarzyna," stamping hard on the r in my name, "how is she doing?"

"I think she's doing fine. I mean, I don't know," I slurred a little.

"What do you mean, you don't know?" Celine spoke faster, and her accent got stronger. "Is she recovering?"

"From what?"

"The dinner!"

"What dinner?"

"You don't know about the dinner?" Celine looked at Mark.

"What dinner?" I frowned. I was annoyed they were being so serious.

"Well, we need to tell her about the dinner," Celine turned to Mark. He nodded, looking tired.

"What fucking dinner?" I asked!

"Shh, she's coming," Mark said, and smiled at Yasmin.

"Are we going to check the desserts?" she asked beaming. She flipped her hair flirtatiously and rubbed her nose.

"There is only one dessert I need," Mark said putting a pack of cigarettes on the table.

"Phew. Boring," Yasmin teased.

"Kate, you smoke too?" he asked. I nodded. "Shall we?"

"Sweetie, want to share a dame blanche?" Celine asked Yasmin as we were getting up.

Mark and I walked out onto the cobblestone street. There was a breeze outside. My temples were pulsating.

"Here's the thing," Mark started, lighting both of our cigarettes.

"The dinner thing."

Mark sighed and took a long drag on his cigarette.

"It happened three months ago. Well, with Yasmin, shit happens *all the time*. I wish Celine would see it." He rolled his eyes and added under his breath, "Fuck, even Yasmin can see it, that's why she called you this time."

"Yasmin came back to Brussels because her parents live here. She needed a refill. She tried looking for work, but with little success. Her mother was still super pissed because of the dance academy, so she turned her down, but the father, well, you know, an only child, his little girl." Mark rolled his eyes again. "He secretly gave her money and as soon as the mother found out, a fight broke out and Yasmin was cut off. She lived off friends and what not for a month. Mostly us, eh? Celine and me. The nerve, I mean… Like, is she giving you any money right now?"

"Money?"

"Yeah, for staying with you, for groceries?"

"No, but…"

"Sheesh. Jesus, you're even worse than her."

"Excuse me? She needs help, and I am happy to…" I fired back.

"Look, Kate, it's fine," he raised his hands. "None of my business. I am more than happy to be rid of her and her sob stories. Okay? Just trying to be fair with you."

"Sure," I mumbled, taking a long drag.

"Anyway, let me finish this latest instalment of Yasmin's never-ending drama," he said, pulling his eyes away from me. I felt like he was annoyed that I wasn't siding with him.

"Eventually, she and the parents made a bargain. If they continued financing her, she would re-enrol in the dance academy." He stubbed out his cigarette and quickly lit a new one. I wasn't smoking mine fast enough; I just held it in my hand like a useless tiny torch.

"They met at a restaurant. The parents were apparently in a good mood." He pushed the words out of his mouth lazily. I could tell that he'd told this story before. Then he made a long pause, glanced behind his back at our restaurant and lowered his voice. "And then, I'm not sure what happened. Honestly. A short circuit in her brain? Or, just Yasmin being *truly* Yasmin."

"She said, and I want to stress here, 'she said', that before coming to the restaurant, she had swallowed half a bottle of sleeping pills. She threw a tantrum, told them she couldn't help herself, that was the only thing that seemed clear to her, yadda-yadda, etc." Mark took a short drag on his cigarette, like a shot of courage.

"It was too much for her old man. He shook and muttered 'you didn't! You must go to the hospital.' Half a minute later he grabbed his chest and slumped over. Dead on the spot." Mark finished the cigarette, took a long breath of fresh air and looked over his shoulder where a group of people were shouting. Dismissing the situation with a frown, he looked down at me. "Now you know. She and the mother haven't spoken since."

"W-wait," I stuttered, "You think she… lied? That she didn't take the pills?"

"What the fuck does it matter? I don't know what happened before *or* after. I know all three of them were taken to hospital that night, but Yasmin didn't tell us more than that. Whether she took them or just said she did – both options are fucked-up. And what's even more fucked-up, is you and Celine caring this much. For fuck's sake!" Mark became more upset than I expected.

"Kate, you know what you have to do, right?"

I couldn't get any air into my lungs. The collar around my throat was too tight and kept getting tighter. Mark's eyes went wobbling, then I realised it wasn't his eyes, it was his head, then I realised it wasn't his head, it was the street.

"Kate!" Mark's voice echoed off into the copper spring sky. I folded forward and vomited on his shoes. After that, everything went cloudy.

* * *

When I think back to dinner I see it in flashes, like burned film tape, zooming in on images of people's faces – Celine's ashy hair, Yasmin's wide pupils, and Mark's frowning eyebrows. I hear long, stretched out sounds, like sirens drawing near and pushing away. Yasmin laughing, skipping and clapping her hands, Mark swearing and cleaning his shoes, Celine running around, paying the check, getting the car, trying to calm everyone, mostly herself.

Keys jangling, keys falling on the floor, Yasmin and I laughing, peeling off our clothes, shoes falling on the floor, *"Shhhh! Hahahhaha"*, water splattering over my face and arms, Yasmin humming to Radiohead, birds chirping outside my window, the wind blowing the curtains in.

I remember nesting in my bed and giggling. Yasmin's smile closing in on me, her hair tickling my cheeks. I remember her belly, cold against mine which was on fire. Her bones, protruding and adjusting, like they wanted to escape Yasmine's tight skin; our hips locked in.

Near dawn, I put my arm on hers, and whispered into the dark, "Yasmin, I want you... to know I know. I know what happened. I will never judge you. I am here for you. We'll make it through it all."

She was silent a long time.

"I didn't ask you to be here for me."

She let me spoon her. I fell asleep quickly, too tired to discuss what had just happened. When I woke up, she was gone.

Dozens of calls went unanswered: I lost count of the times I listened to the same voicemail greeting. In the two agonizing conversations I had with Celine, pleading, crying, shaking, she said she "didn't know what to tell me." Maybe she knew, but was just being kind. I decided to put off trying to understand the lesson I was supposed to learn. I turned away from the prying sun and buried my face in the pillow. It still smelled of Yasmin and I all I wanted was to hold on to that for a few minutes longer.

Katja Knežević is a poet and short story writer. In 2012 she was awarded the first prize at the Sea of Words competition with the short story *Invisible Mother*. In 2014 she won the Croatian national award for young poets with the manuscript *Birches made of glass*. The collection was published in April 2015. She writes in English and Croatian.

Anastasia Cojocaru
TEDDIES

I'm waiting for the metro. By Friday I'm always so exhausted. The metro can't come quick enough. As it pulls into the station, I find myself standing in front of one of the doors. I can see a couple of people in the carriage already, but the corridor in front of me is empty. The door opens and I'm staring into a circle of multi-coloured teddy bears perfectly placed on the floor. A man sits in the centre. He's wearing a coat and hat both covered in teddies. I get on anyway.

Two teddies seem to be midway through a heated discussion. I look to see who's talking.

"*Pourquoi tu ne parles qu'à l'ours en peluche vert? Tu ne me parles plus*", says the blue teddy.

"*Si, je te parle. Je t'apporte des fleurs aussi*".

"*Je ne veux plus te voir, c'est fini!*", the blue teddy continues.

"*Tu ne peux pas m'échapper, mon amour. On finira dans le même sac à la fin de la journée*", the yellow teddy goes.

I am speechless, but can't stop watching.

"*Je demanderai à la peluche dinosaure de me protéger*".

"*Vas-y, demande-lui si elle pourrait aussi trouver ton œil manquant*".

"*C'est quoi, ce bordel? Les autres nounours veulent dormir. Zut!*", a dinosaur teddy intervenes.

The metro stops and someone else gets on. She doesn't seem to want to be around the teddies, I think, as she quickly moves to another part of the carriage. On her way, she knocks the violet teddy from the circle, seemingly by accident. I find myself gasping. There's a pause in the teddies' conversation, and intense staring and frowning from the man. Blue teddy shouts something at her in French that I don't understand. Then, he picks up the fallen teddy and sets it back gently into the circle. The man smiles. The doors close and the teddies carry on their conversation as if nothing had happened.

Anastasia Cojocaru is a queer woman of Romanian heritage. Her poetry is inspired by her memories growing up in post-communist Romania, the time she spent abroad, and Romanian superstitions, myths & folklore. She uses poetry to wrangle meaning from a senseless world and crystallize profound moments into words. Find her @nastiacojocaru on Twitter and Instagram.

Sheila Kinsella
IN MARY SCHOLES' HOUSE

I sit in the armchair facing the window. Mary Scholes stands and stares at me. I feel like I am starring in a film and she is going to tell me how to act. Through the window, I watch as the flashing lights of the ambulance fade into the distance. I blink, but red blobs flicker in my eyes long after the siren has faded.

"Sit there. Don't move," Mary Scholes says. She sits down opposite me.

I've never been this close to her. Dark eyes glare at me through thick spectacles; her eyes remind me of Goldie when he swims up against his bowl. Mary Scholes's brown hair is tall and looks sticky. Mammy says she uses heated rollers and lacquer. Honestly, it doesn't look like it budges. She wears a beige twin set. Rolls of flesh flow over the top of her skirt like the man who advertises tyres on the telly.

Mary Scholes throws stones at cats when they go into her garden, she has a neat pile of pebbles by the front door. She screams at kids, "get off the grass," and never gives our football back. If only she'd throw balls at the cats, I'd be happy.

I smell the newness of carpet. She told Mammy that it's Axminster. I want to lie on the floor and let the soft carpet threads swallow me up. I want to push my fingers into the deep tufts and force them apart, like Jesus parting the sea in the stories at school.

I look up at the wall above the fireplace. Framed photographs of Mary Scholes' son, Denis, fill the space in a higgledy-piggledy way. Flowery wallpaper fills the gaps in-between. In the biggest picture, in the middle, Denis's roly-poly red face rolls over the edge of the frame. His blue eyes squint, struggling to see over his chubby cheeks. A floppy fringe stops just above his eyebrows. Mammy says that Mary Scholes fed Denis so much that he's in a special place now.

My eyes stray to the mantelpiece. There's no insurance company savings clock in Mary Scholes' house. At home, I like to watch Mammy drop coins into the slot and wait to hear the clunk of them dropping to the bottom. In Mary Scholes' house, a glass carriage clock with a funny mixture of letters where the numbers should be, stands on the mantelpiece. I can't see a slot to put the money in.

"Do you want a drink of fizzy pop?" Mary Scholes barks at me.

Silence.

"Cat got your tongue?"

"Yes please," I say, in the hope that she will leave the room and stop watching me. But she's back before I have time to stroke the carpet.

"Don't spill it," she plonks the bottle on a coaster on the coffee table.

At my house we don't have a coffee table. We don't drink coffee. We drink tea; dark, brown, strong tea with each meal.

"Quiet one, aren't you?" Mary Scholes stares at me.

Glug, glug. I gulp the pop.

"They're the worst," Mary Scholes mutters as she straightens the lace cloths covering the arms of her chair.

My legs hurt from sitting so still. I swing them slightly to wake them up. My big toe peeps out of my sock like a small potato. Mary Scholes made me leave my shoes at the back door.

"Watch your feet on that armchair."

I still my feet. I want to snuggle inside the soft armchair. I want to touch all the things in the room. I want to move things around. But most of all, I wonder why Mammy left me here. Did I do something wrong, was I bad?

In my mind I begin to make a list of my naughtiness. 1) I let the cat sleep in my bed. 2) I hid him under the covers. 3) I shook the tomato ketchup bottle until the lid flew off, the ketchup splattering over the white wall. 4) I pushed the loo brush down the toilet so hard it got stuck. The toilet was blocked for a week.

"Take your hands off the arms of my chair," Mary Scholes interrupts my thoughts. I feel her eyes drilling a hole in my head.

I don't know what to do with my hands. I put them under my bottom. They start to warm like when I am grilling toast on a fork in front of the fire.

"Stop that sniffing."

My nose starts to dribble, and I lick my top lip to mop it up.

"Don't you have a hanky?" She pulls a grumpy face and hands me her own crumpled handkerchief. "Here, wipe that nose."

The handkerchief smells musty. I don't want to use it, but I do. When I'm finished, I crumple it up and hand it back to her. She doesn't move.

"Don't be daft, you'll want to use it again," Mary Scholes says.

I look around the room for toys. There aren't any. Maybe Denis doesn't play with toys. I look anywhere but at Mary Scholes.

"What's Santa bringing you this year?" She asks.

"I don't know," I mumble.

"He only gives presents to good girls," she looks down her nose at me.

My eyes start to water. I blink hard to try and make the tears go away. I sniff.

"For goodness sake, stop that sniffing!"

I feel hot. I want to go home. I don't care that Mammy is not there. I want to go home. I need a pee.

"Only babies cry."

The doorbell rings. Mary Scholes gets up to answer the door. It's the Lemonade man. I can see his yellow truck through the net curtains.

"Hello Mary, what'll you have today?" He almost sings at her.

The Lemonade man sells fizzy pop. We don't drink pop. Mammy says there's plenty of water in the tap.

"Hello Peter. We'll have three bottles of Dandelion and Burdock, one Cherryade and one Cream Soda please."

"Right you are then. Back in a jiffy," Peter's voice fades away as he goes to his truck to get the bottles.

"I'll just get my purse." Mary Scholes says as she goes into the kitchen. I am up and out of that front door before Mary Scholes can stop me.

"Get back here!" She screams.

"Hey up chuck, in a hurry?" The Lemonade man opens his arms to try and catch me, but I am too fast.

I tear across the road to our house. As I cross the grass verge, I feel a hot trickle creeping down my leg. I try hard to hold it in. The front door is on the latch. I push hard, the door flies open and I run into the toilet. The seat is cold. I take a deep breath. The relief is instant. It seems to go on forever. I lift my head and look up. In my rush, I didn't close the toilet door and the front door is wide open. Mary Scholes and the Lemonade man stare back at me, mouths agog.

"Well, really!" Mary Scholes marches towards me. "There's a perfectly good toilet in my house!"

My eyes start to fill-up. I bite my lip hard to stop myself from crying. I've barely time to finish up and flush the loo before Mary Scholes grabs my wrist and yanks me out of the house. I hear the click of the lock as she flicks it down, slams the door and drags me across to her place. Her red painted nails dig into my flesh, she doesn't release me until the Lemonade van moves down the street, its bottles rattling in their crates.

"Get in there now!" Mary Scholes roars, pointing at her kitchen.

I rub my wrist, sniff, and then wipe my tears with the back of my hand.

"Wash them hands!" Mary Scholes switches the tap on and points at the green soap.

"I'll get some tea on," she takes a tin of baked beans out of the kitchen cupboard.

She cuts two slices of bread and puts them in the toaster. They pop up, she slathers them with butter and places them on an old plate. Seeing the beans being poured on top of the toast makes me think of jellied frogspawn tumbling out of a jam jar when we play in the stream. I don't want to eat them now, thinking of those baby tadpoles. Will Mammy ever come back?

"There. Eat that." Mary Scholes puts the plate down hard in front of me. I almost gag on the first mouthful, but daren't not eat. Mary Scholes whisks the plate away the second I'm finished, washes it and puts it back in the cupboard. I dab my finger over the tiny orange lake of baked bean sauce on the table and wipe it under the chair.

Mary Scholes doesn't want me in her house, and I do not want to be here.

"Pudding," Mary Scholes slides a bowl overflowing with Neapolitan ice cream over the table towards me.

I stare down at the dish and up at her.

"Go on then! Eat it!" She implores. "Bet you don't get that at home." I manage the chocolate part and pause for a breath.

"Denis loves Neapolitan," Mary Scholes actually smiles, displaying massive yellow teeth large that are sharp like a dog's.

I struggled, but manage to force down the last spoonful. I stayed very still. Gurgling noises coming from my tummy.

"Here's some toffees for later," she placed a clutch of sweets into my hand.

The telephone rings loudly from down the hall.

"Newtown 3239, lady of the house speaking," Mary Scholes said.

"Yes." Pause. "Fine." Pause. "Good." Mary Scholes replied. She turned to me, "Your dad is coming to collect you to take you to the hospital. Have some more pop before you go."

The hospital was big and scary with corridors reeking of vinegar. Our footsteps echoed as we walked.

Mammy is in a room with lots of tired looking ladies sitting-up in bed. She looks different somehow, I don't know why.

"Astór, my little treasure, come here," Mammy smiles and beckons me to her and lifts the bedcovers. "Meet your little sister."

The baby is like a very red doll, with clumps of blonde hair and a crinkly face. I step forward for a closer look. I feel a sudden lurch in my chest and wretch the entire contents of my belly on the floor.

That is how we first met, my sister and me.

Brussels based Irish writer **Sheila Kinsella's** short stories draw inspiration from childhood memories and everyday life. An avid people watcher, Sheila is blessed with abundant natural curiosity and lures the reader into a shrewdly observed world via imagery and comedy. She graduated with an MA in Creative Writing from Lancaster University, United Kingdom, in 2017.

Klavs Skovsholm
A PIRATE PARROT CHRISTMAS

"Pirate Jaco, Commander of the proud ship *The Flying Birdcage*, at your service!" Jaco the Parrot yelled in his coarse voice. He stuck his grey, feathered head over the side of his vessel. *The Flying Birdcage* was circling above a polar bear drifting across the open sea on a large ice floe.

The bear stood up, confused at the black hull of the vessel with forty cannons and black sails hovering above his head. But not just any ship, a real pirate ship! The bear looked very thin and downcast.

"Which way to the North Pole, Sir?" the parrot asked.

The bear arched its eyebrows in surprise. In these areas, everyone knew where North was!

"Yes, this may seem a curious question, but our compass is broken," the Commander offered as an explanation to the bear who gave no response.

"Which way to the North Pole, Sir?" the parrot asked again, raising his voice in irritation.

When the bear moved its snout towards a point on the Southern horizon, Jaco mistook it for North.

"Thank you, Sir! Much obliged!" he continued, turning to his crew of sparrows. "Weigh anchor! Need to gain altitude. And set course due North, first officer Crow!" The officer did as he was told, immediately crowing commands to the sparrows.

"But Captain, we cannot just leave the poor bear behind," tweeted one of the sparrows.

"No time to lose, I'm afraid. He knows how to swim!"

"But Captain, we're on the open sea..." Before the sparrow had said this, Captain Jaco lunged forward and kicked him over the side of the ship. He landed next to the bear who began to sniff the feathers of the petrified bird.

With the wind vigorously catching its dark sails, The Flying Birdcage swiftly gained altitude. The sparrow and bear could do nothing but watch the stern of the black vessel sailing due South on the winds with the grace of an albatross.

"What's wrong with sparrows nowadays, Crow?"

"Aye, Captain."

"In the old days, they would do what they were told. Now they twitter as if they were parrots!" He laughed at his own joke while the sparrows around him ducked their heads and got on with their work.

"Aye, Captain" Crow answered, nodding approvingly.

"Crow, our next stop is the North Pole, I feel sure of it," Jaco continued triumphantly. "This time Santa will not get away! I must get there early."

"Aye, Captain!"

"I will commandeer his sleigh and take him hostage! All children around the world will empty their piggy banks to pay the ransom and just in time to save Christmas. I can buy a rainforest and be King of the Jungle! Think of it!"

"Aye, Captain."

"Crow, I want more speed! Let's pick up some wind!"

Crow did as commanded. *The Flying Birdcage* lunged forward, taking the sails almost to the point of tearing apart.

"Yes, Crow! Now, this is what I call sailing!" The pirate parrot called out from his high perch. He watched the blurred landscapes of snowy mountains fly under the keel of his boat. Jaco sat captivated by these views for the longest time, before it dawned on him that something was amiss.

"Something's wrong, Crow! These countries are getting lower and lower!"

"If the countries are low, it must be the Low Countries, Sir!"

"Low Countries? We're heading the wrong way! Pigeon brain! Stop! Immediately!"

With a fearful frenzy, the sparrows struck the sails, bringing *The Flying Birdcage* to an almost complete stop over a town with small narrow houses crisscrossed by canals. The pirate ship touched down stealthily on a wide canal.

The moon was out and the townspeople were nowhere in sight, but for a drunkard who came cycling along, his bicycle swaying dangerously left and right. He cried out, lost his balance and drove right into the canal the moment after noticing the dark silhouette of the vessel next to him, twenty cannons pointing his way.

"Take a look, Crow, can that human swim?"

"Aye, Captain."

Jaco was busy pointing his spyglass in the direction of a barge with four old fashioned lanterns, which was heading in the ship's direction.

"Now what have we got here? A barge that moves by itself? What is this? Could it be? Yes, it must be!" The parrot lowered the spyglass and barked,

"Prepare for boarding, Crow! Turn the vessel and prepare the cannons."

"Aye, Captain!"

The ship turned to block the barge, its loaded canons rolled out and along the side of the deck, sparrows with black headscarves and angled daggers clutched in their beaks, readying themselves for an assault.

"Throw out the ropes!" the captain commanded.

Each rope had a large hook at the end which would allow them to bring the barge up against the side of the ship. As the pirates approached, two characters onboard the barge and their white donkey with abnormally long ears, stood still watching as the Commander was lowered onto the barge, in a swing over the side of the vessel, showing off his red tail in the process.

"Good evening! I'm Commander Jaco! I do not come in peace!"

Jaco let his eyes wander from the old man with his long white beard and his red robe and pointed hat, to his tall companion whose face and clothes were covered in dust. The old man had a gilded stick in his hand. The white donkey, which had stood behind them, walked up to the parrot.

"You need to wash! How come you are so dirty?" He asked the tall man irritably, ignoring the donkey.

"Climbing chimneys," the man answered. The pirate nodded, turning to the old man.

"Santa, you should have your companion clean himself!" he barked coarsely before he spat on the deck.

The old man cocked his head in surprise.

"My name is not Santa," he replied firmly. "My name is Nicholas and this is my friend Peter".

"You're not Santa?" Jaco said.

"No, my name is Nicholas – and we have come from Spain. Santa is my famous American cousin."

"Why are you here?"

The old man fell quiet with a hesitant look on his face. Peter stole a glance over his shoulder towards the doors to the cargo hold below. Jaco pushed past them and threw open one of the doors.

"Bring some light!" he ordered. The donkey came gaily forward and let his nose shine.

The parrot stared at the donkey, stunned.

"Don't worry," the donkey said, "I'm a magic donkey. I've seen my friend Rudolf do this and I thought it was rather cool, so I taught myself how to do it!" The donkey smiled broadly and swung his ears from side to side.

"Right." Jaco said, shaking his head in disbelief. Using light from the donkey's nose, he leaned forward to inspect the hold.

"Oranges! Oranges! The cargo hold is full of oranges!" He cried out in anger. "Where are the presents, Santa?"

He looked menacingly at the old man who came forward with his stick pointed at him.

"What's in that one?" Jaco continued and made for the other door in the deck.

"Those are just Santa's pre-deliveries," the donkey happily jabbered on, but was cut short as Nicholas hit him over the head with his stick. Nicholas strode forward and took up position at the door to the hold. Jaco sensed that Peter had moved too, but he was faster, flew past him and got on to the swing.

"Hoist me up!"

The sparrows above immediately pulled on the ropes and Jaco sped upwards.

"Get the cannons ready, Crow! Use the big seeds! Santa's not going to get away!"

Below him on the barge, he noticed that the old man in the red robe was swinging his stick in circles over his head, creating a thick mist in the process. Within seconds, the barge had disappeared behind a curtain of fog.

"Crow, send up an emergency flare so we can see what's going on!"

"Aye, Captain!"

Moments later the fog began to lift and, in the red glare of the flare, Jaco saw that the barge had been transformed into a tall ship as large as his own, now lifting off the canal with all sails set.

"A ghost ship! *The Flying Dutchman*!" one of the sparrows shrieked. "We're doomed!"

"No one's abandoning ship!" the pirate parrot yelled. "The first one to do so will be plucked alive! Crow, chain down anyone attempting to fly away!"

"My pleasure, Captain."

"Weigh anchor! Set all sails! Engage pursuit!"

As soon as the anchor was free of the water, a strong side wind caught the sails. *The Flying Birdcage* lifted with a jolt, swaying wildly and headed straight for the side of the canal. The drunkard, who was now back on land, threw himself to the ground as the vessel came straight at him. Crow narrowly avoided a collision with the nearest house. At the last moment, he managed to make the ship climb so steeply that *The Flying Birdcage* only knocked off the chimney.

"Excellent, Crow! Nothing like a little wind-water rafting!" Jaco yelled as he was struggling to get back on his perch.

Crow was pale and quiet. There was not a single tweet from the sparrows.

"Now, where did they go? I see them! I see them!" the pirate parrot cried and pointed with his spyglass.

Crow took up pursuit, pushing the vessel so hard that her masts cracked and groaned. They were now positioning themselves next to the other vessel. Peter was steering, and on deck was a crew of meerkats baring their sharp teeth at the sparrows.

"Where's the old man?"

Then he saw Nicholas who signalled with his stick. The cannons thundered. Now oranges flew straight at them. On impact, they splattered all over the place. Some sparrows were swept overboard.

"Fire!" Jaco yelled at the top of his lungs. The deck under his feet shook violently as the cannons spat out a hailstorm of heavy seeds, resulting in another wave of oranges coming their way.

"Fire! More seeds!"

"Captain!"

"Not now, Crow!"

"But Captain, look ahead!"

The loud sound of fast approaching engines suddenly dwarfed the noise of the firing cannons. Jaco looked ahead.

"Sharp turn to the left, Crow! Turn left!"

Crow threw *The Flying Birdcage* to the left just before a huge blue and white aircraft thundered past, tearing most of her sails apart with its jet stream.

"Fly! Fly!" some of the sparrows cried before they abandoned ship just as the vessel rapidly lost altitude.

"Mayday, Captain!" cried Crow.

The Commander ignored him.

"Cowards! Cowards!" Jaco shouted, holding on to a rope, as he watched the sparrows fly off.

The Flying Birdcage was wildly spinning towards the ground, but Crow managed to somewhat control its descent by using the few sails left. Jaco watched with the wind pressing against his face as dark fields below rapidly came closer and closer.

"Prepare for impact, Captain!" Crow managed to shout before the vessel touched down with a big bang and skidded forward, bumping up and down and stopping in front of a munching cow. Part of the ship's hull had caved in.

Crow turned grey. Jaco jumped off the ship to inspect the damage. He could immediately see that *The Flying Birdcage* would need massive repairs. The sight of her brought tears to his eyes.

"Crow, I believe we've got work to do," he said with a sigh, but he got no further as he suddenly heard the jingling of bells. Jaco turned to see where the jingling was coming from. What at first appeared to be a dark object turned out to be a sleigh drawn by a multitude of reindeer. One of them was flashing his nose light as the sleigh came to a standstill, hovering above his head. A man with a white beard stuck his head over the side of the sleigh.

"Ho, ho, ho! Merry Christmas! Merry Christmas! I'm Santa Claus, Commander of *The Flying Sleigh*, at your service!" the man yelled in his deep, happy voice. Jaco said nothing.

"Ho, ho, ho! I'm early this year. Off to rescue a bear and a sparrow! Better luck next time!" The sleigh flew off.

"Next year, Santa! Next Year!" Jaco yelled after the man. The taste of defeat was hard to swallow, but he now had twelve months to make *The Flying Birdcage* as good as new and devise a bigger, better plan to capture Santa.

Klavs Skovsholm works as a lawyer for the European Union. He published two historical novels *Golden Fields* and *At the Bay* set in South Africa during the Boer war. Together, with South African foundation Stigting vir Bemagtiging Deur Afrikaans, he has published several multilingual school books for children *Die Kokerboom*, *Robbie die rowwe Rot* and *Fatima*, including braille versions.

Patrick ten Brink
THE CARP AND THE MAGPIE

The Carp and the Magpie *was first published by Night Picnic Press and is included here with thanks.*

Centuries ago, a giant carp swam through the slow moving streams of the moss lined cedar forests of Japan. She had bright green eyes in a face like fresh snow and her fins and tail glistened like silver. Orange patches adorned her belly and sides, though her back was black. She cut through the water in silence, her two long barbels drawing lines on its surface.

One night, she poked her head out of the water and gazed upon the heavens. She sang – her mouth wide open, her gills vibrating. Slow, deep notes rippled through the water and soon fish, big and small, gathered to hear her.

A magpie, perched on a moss-covered pine branch above, cocked his head so that one of his deep, black eyes could watch the forming school of fish.

With barbels rising and falling, the carp sang of the Red Phoenix who resides in the Heavens.

> "The Phoenix is the noblest
> and most magical of birds.
> It dies, but lives forever,
> reborn again and again from her ashes."

The magpie ruffled his feathers noisily and squawked, "Magpies are as clever as any Phoenix."

"Clever perhaps, but who has heard of a wise magpie?" The carp pursed her lips.

"Oh, wise carp who claims to read the stars. In the heavens, there are two celestial fish, joined at the tail. I wonder, can you tell us why this is so?"

"Together they can swim up any stream, brook, even the fiercest of rapids. But swimming against each other, they would never leave the quiet ponds and never reach the stars."

The school of fish nodded, and the magpie asked, "If there are two fish in the sky, why do we see only one carp in these waters? Where is the other?"

The carp was silent, scanning the stars before replying, "The fish in the sky are two but one."

The magpie said, "Nice answer, but you are still only one."

"As you are one on that branch," said the carp, before swimming away to a quiet pond. She slept and dreamt of meeting another fish like her. Maybe there were two as in the sky, maybe more.

The carp awoke at sunrise and poked her head out of the water. The school of fish had dispersed. The magpie, still perched above, said, "Why did nature only make one of you?" He sidled up to the end of the branch as it bent close to carp, and whispered, "Don't you ever feel alone?"

The carp closed her mouth and stared at the last stars fading in the morning light. The magpie's words took hold like a water louse itching its way into her mind.

"Oh, wise and lonely carp. No constellations honour my kind in the skies, but as I fly, I discover the secrets of the land. If you like, I can show you things you've never seen."

The carp opened her mouth but said nothing.

"I'll show you a secret," said the magpie, spreading his wings wide. "Behold." There was a line of black Kanji along one feather. "I can help you understand things you have only dreamt of."

"And what do I need to do in return for the wisdom you promise?" asked the carp.

"Sing me the songs of the stars as we travel the lands. I too have dreams, to be the songbird of the skies."

"That is a request worthy of the Phoenix," said the carp.

"Our trip will take three days and three nights. Meet me at the next still waters." The magpie said before flying away.

As the first stars emerged in the darkening sky, the carp reached the next still waters. There she saw a frail old man carrying a bowl, a brush and an ink stick. The magpie was perched on his shoulder. The man sat on a large flat rock at the edge of the pond just in front of the carp, and tightened his coat against the evening breeze.

The magpie settled next to the man's feet and said to the carp, "Sing the constellation of the stars that befits this poet, and he will write on your scales."

The carp gazed at the heavens, seeking one of the twenty-eight constellations that was right for the poet. She opened her mouth and out came rich, deep tones of the constellation of the bear – with its pointed nose, great arching back, thick black fur, and powerful claws.

As the last note faded, the old man said, "Oh wise, kind, carp, you have offered me the fierceness and resistance of the bear. I should make it through the harsh winter now. What can I offer you in return?"

The carp scanned the stars, her eyes alighting on the constellation of the two fish. She murmured, "I am alone under the stars. I wish to feel loneliness no longer."

"As in the stars," said the old man, grinding the ink stick in the bowl. He raised his brush, "I am an old man, but I hope that I am worthy of returning your favour. For that, I need your tail."

Arching her body, the carp lifted her tail above the water.

The poet dried carp's scales with a cloth and drew a black and a white fish on one side of the tailfin, joined as yin and yang. These he encircled with a line of words, then another, and another, until the tailfin was completely covered in spiralling sentences.

"You are already two together as one, only you have forgotten. These poems of night and day will remind you. Keep your tail out of the water this night, and the words will never leave you. Do not press the circle with the two fish. Remember the constellations of the heavens — celestial fish are joined as one by the tail, release them, and they become two, able to swim in opposing directions." He bowed and walked into the forest.

"Become two?" wondered the carp as she plunged her face deeper into the water, careful to keep her tail in the air. She repeated, "You are already two together," with each beat of her side fins.

The night was long. When she felt the first rays of sun warm her tail, the carp drifted to the depths of the pond and slept. In her dreams, she pressed her tail against a rock and became two.

She woke, happy, yet troubled. She resurfaced, each poem still adorning her tail.

"We should go," said the magpie from the other side of the pond. A pile of black berries lay next to his clawed feet. He flicked one berry after the other into the water. Carp gobbled them up before the two set-off again.

As the sun set on another day of travel, the exhausted carp reached a pond surrounded by thick-stemmed bamboo. There was magpie standing among the fresh shoots, a cricket in his beak, which he promptly swallowed. "Crickets are supposed to bring good luck," said the magpie.

"I'm not sure… it was meant… that way," murmured the carp.

"At least I don't eat cicadas."

"Good; it is said they house the souls of poets."

"Maybe I should eat them?"

"Magpies that eat cicadas have been known to turn into crows," warned the carp.

The magpie snapped up another cricket, and said, "Another unlucky one." He flew off, calling back, "I will find the next spirit of the woods for you. Eat now, my friend, and rest."

The carp sank to the bottom of the pond and grazed on the water plants, resisting the urge to press the drawing of the yin-yang fish. She swam over the plants time and again, her tail coming ever closer to their stems.

A silver-haired woman in a faded kimono emerged from the bamboo wood. She carried a staff in one hand and the magpie hopped along next to her. She struggled to reach the side of the pond, a hard, tap-tap-tap of her staff as she walked onto a dark pockmarked rock. She looked through milky cataracts at the rippling waters.

The carp said, "When the stars are out, I will find a constellation and sing for you."

The woman nodded, leant on her staff, and waited.

When the stars emerged, the carp sang of the constellation of the Phoenix, with its starry eyes and spread wings, flying up to the heavens — the carp's notes filled the sky like a rumbling storm, rising higher and higher, until they waned, dying down to a whisper, to a murmur, to silence, only to re-emerge as a delicate, high-pitched shrill, and eventually into a striding, joyful melody.

The old woman listened intently, with her eyes closed.

When the song finished, the woman bowed and said to the carp, "You offer me hope to be reborn. I will offer you the same." She took out pots of coloured powders and two paintbrushes. Squinting at the carp, she said, "Look at the colours on your scales; you are blessed with the colours of a whole school of fish. Lend me your tail."

When she saw the tail with its black and silvery-white yin-yang carp and the poems, she smiled. "You have given a great gift to the first master, and he has returned the honour. He saw that you are wise and kind enough for two. If what the magpie says is true, you are wise and kind enough for four, maybe more."

On the other side of the tail she painted a red-orange fish and a blue one. "You have the sun and the sky in you now, as well as day and night. May this be the thanks you are looking for, noble carp." She then encircled the new yin-yang with her own poems written in green ink. "I give you the poems of nature too. Thank you for your song."

That night the carp struggled to keep her tail out of the water. Several times she battled sleep's clutches and each time she won. With the first rays of the sun, she sank to the bottom to rest. This time she dreamed that she became a shoal of a hundred carp, each speaking at the same time, fighting to be heard, bubbles disturbing the tranquility of the water. She couldn't understand a word that was spoken.

The carp woke-up when a pebble bumped her head, then another, and a third. The carp struggled to the surface where she found the magpie nudging another stone towards the water's edge.

"What are you doing?" she asked.

"A lazy carp can never truly be a wise carp, my friend," said the magpie.

The carp sighed. "Is this quest wise? In my dreams—"

"Listen to the wisdom of the last spirit of the forest," said the magpie, "and you will be a truly wise carp and no longer feel alone."

The carp opened her mouth to talk, but it was too late, the magpie had flown off. She beat her tail sluggishly, making the barest of ripples.

The stars were already out when she reached the base of a waterfall. The magpie was perched on a glistening rock, pecking blueberries. He said, "She is up above."

"I am too weak to go any further. My tail trembles with exhaustion."

"Berries and lotus flowers await you. Brave the waters. You can do this."

Exhausted, the carp shook her head from side to side. "I cannot."

The magpie said, "You have black patches on your sides. Show that you merit these marks of courage and persistence. You wouldn't wish to disappoint the many fish who await your return."

The carp sighed and dove under, the fresh water from the fall sweeping through her gills. She let herself be pushed back, then whipped her tail again and again, making her way through the harsh jet of water, eventually over the rock, all the way scratching her belly, until she landed in the calm waters at the top. Her underside stung, but she was too exhausted to speak. She floated, aching all over.

"Oh, wise carp, you have done it!"

"What have I done?"

A young woman with long, unkempt black hair, stumbled towards the pool, zigzagging through the rocks. Her shoulders were hunched forward, her legs and arms twisted. Her purple kimono was torn. She winced as she sat down and dipped her feet in the water.

"Time to sing," demanded the magpie.

The carp scanned the heavens for the right constellation. It was not an easy choice. The woman walked sideways like a crab through the rocks, but what is the point of singing of the crab when she already knows its dance?

The carp saw Andromeda, the Chained Maiden, leaning back in the heavens, arms and legs pulled back at odd angles. The carp listened to the stars and repeated the constellation's song. The notes were harsh, broken, edgy, but, little by little, they softened and flowed into a melody that spread through the air like perfume from a lotus flower.

As the woman listened, she relaxed, her arms and legs gradually straightening.

When the song was complete, the weary carp closed her eyes.

When she opened them, the magpie was perched on the woman's right shoulder. The woman's hunched back was gone. Her arms and legs were straight, the twisted neck long and graceful. Her grimace had become a beautiful smile. She said, "O kind carp, you have unchained me. Name your wish."

"My wish?"

"The carp and I have travelled many days and nights together," said the magpie. "We are like family now. I can speak for her."

Belly stinging, weary and lost, the carp struggled to find words for what she wanted to say.

The magpie intervened, "She yearns for greater wisdom, and dreams of no longer being alone. These are two wishes, I know. But she deserves two, if not more. Look at her scales. The gods have graced her with the many colours of the rainbow."

The young woman studied the carp and said, "Yes, she is one, but has the gifts of many." She crouched next to the carp, "Honour your wishes, I can. But the path to wisdom is not easy." She ran her fingers along the carp's back. "Is that what you want?"

"Forgive me; my belly burns and my mind is numb," said the carp, "please, a moment to ponder the question."

"Can you really do it, Andromeda?" asked the magpie. "Can you transform me too? I dream of being a Phoenix!"

The woman laughed. "I can only grant a full wish to one, and it is for the carp. Are wisdom and the end of loneliness your wish?"

Her voice was like the ululation of the waters, laughter in the splashing waterfalls. The carp nodded. "And I want to go home to share what I have learnt."

"So be it," said the woman. She reached into the water and picked up the carp, one hand under the dripping belly, the other holding the tail. She gazed into carp's eyes and sang a poem. Each syllable made carp's scales vibrate and sing. "When you are many, you will still be one. Remember that." The woman kissed the carp's head and returned her to the water. Carp's tail pressed against the woman's hand, her fingers touching the yin and yang circles. The carp shook and shuddered. The green writing around her tail unravelled and snaked up to her lips, the black poems spread across her body and under her scales.

The magpie flew down and settled on a rock and cawed, "One mouth is not enough for all those words on the carp's lips."

In the pool below there was not one carp, not two, but four – one black with an orange belly, a silver one, a red and white carp, and an olive-green and blue one.

"You are transformed like the Phoenix," said Andromeda, "reborn to learn anew. I wish you luck. You have chosen a path few would have the courage to follow."

The magpie cawed, "Oh, magnificent, wise carp. You are now not one but four. You are the Phoenix of the waters, reborn. And never again alone."

To the carp with an orange belly, magpie said, "You have the wisdom of overcoming the struggle and bear the marks of your pain. You are the night, and that is your time to share your poems."

He turned to the white carp on his left, "You hold the sun on your back. You are the sunrise and sunset, and that is when you can whisper your wisdom."

To the green-blue carp on his right, he said, "You are the voice of nature and the sky."

"Now, what are you?" asked the magpie to a silver carp swimming behind the others, her baleful eyes fixed on him. "Silver carp, you are our mirror. You can never speak, but those who want your wisdom need only to decipher the writing on your scales."

"What a marvellous gift. Together you will become ever wiser, never lonely, and…" the magpie squawked, "as a gift for the rest of us, each part of you a little more modest. I feel better already."

The four carps' mouths poked out the water, their heads swinging back and forth, and eight unblinking eyes staring at each other.

"You have what you asked for my friend, my friends," said the carp. "It is time to go home. And remember, you four are one."

Because it was day, the black carp was silent. As it was not sunrise or sunset, the red and white one was quiet. The green-blue carp stared at the cedar forest rising along the banks of the stream and she too remained silent. Silver carp swam close to the magpie, black letters emerging from under the scales, writing out: "What have I done? What have you done?"

The magpie cawed. "I have fulfilled your wishes. Each of you four can learn anew now, and you will become truly wise once you four learn to be as one. You will thank me one day."

More writing flashed along silver carp's scales, "You speak in riddles! How do we share our wisdom if one of us speaks the night, the other only at dawn and dusk, one remains quiet in awe of the beauty of nature, and I can only speak through words which none can read but man and magpie?"

"I am your friend; I will share your wisdom and words with the others. I can wake at night, sing at dawn and dusk, and read the writing on your side," said the magpie. "I can help you four remain one. Now follow me home; many fish await your words. It is all downstream from here. I'll show you the way. Trust me; I am the bright bird of the woods." He spread his wings. A blue sheen covered his black feathers.

The four carp opened and closed their mouths as one, their barbels vibrating up and down, but not one uttered a word. The magpie cocked his head, blinked, and flew off, singing of the stars.

Patrick ten Brink writes fiction and poetry whenever he is not writing non-fiction on environmental matters. His ghost story, *Amelia Borgiotti*, was published by the Coffin Bell Journal, and *The Taken* received Honourable Mention by Glimmer Train. His poem, *Zen Garden, Kyoto*, was one seven winners of the Dreamers Creative Writing Haiku Context. Patrick is currently putting the final touches to his fantasy trilogy, *The Guardians of the Tides*.

Jeannette Cook
DEER OF EUROPE

Deer of Europe, you do well to hide,
to put yourself into spaces
no one can find, where no one
can find you out. I know you exist

in the dark corners of the forest;
I know you exist in plain sight.
I know you by sound and by lack of it.
I know you by what binds –

Stillness, and being that stillness.
Darkness, and holding to it.
Deer of Europe,
you need not show yourselves to me.

It's enough for you to be here,
Enough that you've let me near,
so close I can feel the moment
just before you bound away.

MAELBEEK STATION, SHORTLY AFTERWARD

Absorbed in my phone, I almost forget
to look. And it would be easy to miss,
black panels line the platforms on both sides
making it hard to see anything but rubble;

the kind that might come from any restoration.
Nothing special. Nothing for Facebook.
Nothing worth showing the friend who,
that March morning, emerged with blood and worse

all over his wool coat. He'd loved that coat,
he told me, but left it there: an offering
to whatever gods he owed, and has not been back.

Since the attack he commutes to work by bike.
"It may sound trite," he says, "but I'll be damned
if they'll get any more of my wardrobe."

STILL HERE

I am still here. Not still in the sense
of not having left, or of not having
overstayed, but still as in how water

is still, so that unless you know
where to look, you might think
there is nothing happening.

When you say the words
put the accent on "still" not "here."
When you say "water,"

think of the heron standing
knee-deep in a pond
that you would swear is stagnant.

And yet it brings him fish.
I am that kind of still here.

A native of Royal Oak, Michigan, **Jeannette Cook** has lived in Brussels for 20 years. Her literary city guide to Brussels was published on eatthispoem.com. When she's not writing, you can find her on her yoga mat or at English open mic events in town. Follow Jeannette on Instagram @ifitstuesday.

PRODUCTION TEAM

The Circle 19: a Brussels Anthology would not be possible without the contributions of the following:

Patrick ten Brink, page 181

Kevin Dwyer writes short stories, novels and film scripts, lately as a member of the collaborative Punchdog Productions. His story *Candy* was adapted into the short film *O-Zone* in 2003, and his script *Doing It for Marilyn* is being made into a short film, to be directed by Kevork Aslanyan. He is currently finalizing his novel *Fatlands*, a work of speculative fiction.

Jay Harold, page 71

Cynthia Huijgens received her MEd Art from the University of Minnesota, Minneapolis, and uses the tagline *'art educator exploring write ideas'*. In 2016, she was selected for AWP's Writer to Writer Mentorship Program and graduated from Simon Fraser University's, The Writers Studio Online, in 2017. Cynthia published *My Grandmother's Memoir* in 2018 and is currently Creative Director, Idle Time Press.

Adalbert Jahnz's first name is a dactyl. He writes poems about men in suits.

Mimi Kunz is an artist-writer working with ink and paper. Her art took her to Scotland and Vietnam. Her poems and stories have appeared in performances and magazines. After a post-

MA at the Art Academy Karlsruhe, Germany, Mimi moved to Brussels, where she founded 'Something Beautiful', a festival for visual arts and poetry.

Niamh Moroney, page 44

Ross Noble lives and works in Brussels as a conference interpreter. He is currently working on his debut novel, *The Wisher*, a young adult fantasy set in his native Scotland about a teenager struggling to come to terms with being different.

Antoinette Naomi Reddick is an author, self-development trainer, activist and social anthropologist currently living in Belgium. Her current focus is on global activism and working towards bridging the gap between ethical and cultural divides through literature and artistic expression, developmental research into environmental concerns, and constructing platforms that propagate widespread shift on a social and global scale.

Ocean Smets is a published author of poems, flash fiction and nonfiction. He is launching his second social sci-fi novel *Wheelgasm*, a short story named *The Pavilion*, and an anthology of poems called *Dancing Verses*.

Alexandros Yannis, page 128

SHARE THE CIRCLE 19 WITH FAMILY & FRIENDS!

A big thank you for purchasing *The Circle 19: a Brussels Anthology*. We know you could have picked any number of anthologies to read but you chose ours.

If you enjoyed reading *The Circle 19: a Brussels Anthology*, we invite you to share reviews by posting to Facebook, Twitter, and Instagram. Additionally, posting a review on Amazon or Goodreads, etc. helps spread the word to a wider audience.

If you want to stay in touch or follow the latest news, please visit BWC at

https://brusselswriterscircle.wordpress.com

Thank you again for supporting The Brussels Writers' Circle. See you next year!

Lightning Source UK Ltd.
Milton Keynes UK
UKHW010840191019
351913UK00002B/59/P